Painting the Rainbow

AMY GORDON

Holiday House / New York

Library of Congress Cataloging-in-Publication Data
Gordon, Amy, 1949–
Painting the rainbow / Amy Gordon. — First edition.
pages cm
Summary: During Holly and Ivy's annual month-long visit at the family's New Hampshire lake
house in 1965, the distance that seems to be growing between the thirteen-year-old cousins
fades when they accidentally uncover hints of a family secret dating back to World War II.
ISBN 978-0-8234-2525-9 (hardcover)
[1. Cousins—Fiction. 2. Friendship—Fiction. 3. Secrets—Fiction. 4. Family
problems—Fiction. 5. Family life—New Hampshire—Fiction. 6. Japanese
Americans—Evacuation and relocation, 1942–1945—Fiction. 7. New Hampshire—
History—20th century—Fiction.] I. Title.
PZ7.G65Pai 2014
[Fic]—dc23
2013020999

For the path
between the houses

The Greenwood Family Tree

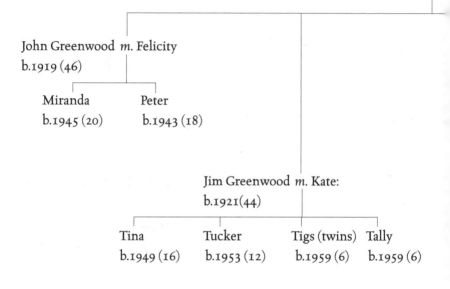

Ted Greenwood *m.*
b.1895 (70)

John Greenwood *m.* Felicity
b.1919 (46)

Miranda
b.1945 (20)

Peter
b.1943 (18)

Jim Greenwood *m.* Kate:
b.1921(44)

Tina
b.1949 (16)

Tucker
b.1953 (12)

Tigs (twins)
b.1959 (6)

Tally
b.1959 (6)

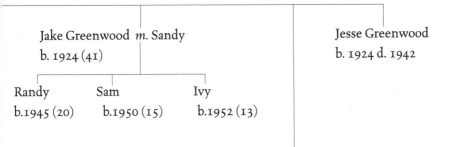

Georgia (Gigi)
b.1897 (68)

Jake Greenwood *m.* Sandy
b. 1924 (41)

Jesse Greenwood
b. 1924 d. 1942

Randy
b.1945 (20)

Sam
b.1950 (15)

Ivy
b.1952 (13)

Jenny Greenwood *m.* Mike Swanson
b. 1926 (39)

Holly
b.1952 (13)

Kiyoshi Mori
b. 1923–d.1965
(age 19 at the
time he met
the Greenwoods)

Ivy's diary

Randy acted so crazy tonight. At supper he said, "Dad, I want to know things you've never told us. Like where Uncle Jesse was when he died in the war, and was he in the army or the navy, or what?"

When he said Uncle Jesse's name, I thought my heart was going to stop. Mom sort of gasped and said, "Randy, you know better," and Sam muttered, "He's got to be joking."

Dad's face turned bright red, and he said, "There's nothing to know about him."

Randy said, "I don't think that's true, and I don't understand why we're not supposed to talk about him. He was your *brother*— your *twin* brother."

Dad exploded then, banging his fist down on the table, making Mom and Sam and me jump. He roared, "That's enough," and he got up and left the room.

Mom said, "Randy—why would you ask such a thing?" and Sam said, "You never know when to keep your mouth shut," and Randy said, "It's not a crime to want to know what happened to my uncle," and Sam said, "Don't you think if Dad wanted you to know he'd tell you?"

Randy stared at him. "You think something *did* happen to him—out of the ordinary, I mean."

Sam turned bright red then, too, and started picking the wax drips off one of the candles on the table. "I didn't say that."

"Stop making a mess," said Mom, and I got up and left the table and came up here to my room. The last thing I want to hear right now is everyone fighting with each other. Thanksgiving was bad enough. Dad was in such a terrible mood, picking on me and Sam and Mom, and he got so mad at Randy that dinner got ruined. I don't know why Randy always has to bring up dangerous topics when we're all sitting down together.

Ivy's diary
Thursday, July 22, 1965

For the first time in my life I am wondering how it was for Dad to
lose a twin brother. It just never occurred to me before. I feel bad
that I never thought about it before, but when you are little you don't
think about things like that. Ever since I turned thirteen in April, I
notice things more. I don't like it. I wish I could turn off my brain.

I guess I don't blame Randy for being curious about Uncle
Jesse. He is such a mystery.

I never even knew Dad had a twin brother until I was eight
years old, and I was at Otter Lake house as usual for our family
vacation. Holly and I found an old photograph of Uncle Jesse under
one of the beds in the Tower Room. It was stuck in a board between
the wall and the floor. We brought it down to the living room
where all the aunts and uncles and Grandpa and Gigi were sitting
around after supper. We ran over to Gigi and showed her the picture
because we thought she could tell us who it was.

I'll never forget how she put a hand up to her heart, and
Grandpa, who was sitting next to her, said, "I don't want to see that,"
and Gigi scooped the photograph out of our hands and tucked it
away somewhere.

And Holly, who has always been braver than me, said, "Why?"

Grandpa barked, "It's enough that I said so!" Grandpa never,
ever yells. It was so unexpected, and Holly and I thought we had
done something really wrong, and we both started crying. I don't
remember Mom being there, but Holly's mom, Aunt Jenny, took us
out of the room. She told us about Uncle Jesse. He had been Dad's
twin, and her brother, too, of course. He died in World War II. The
whole family was really sad when it happened, and Gigi took it
very hard, but Grandpa totally broke down. Aunt Jenny said it was
because terrible things had happened to Grandpa in World War I,
and Jesse's dying brought them all back.

So then Holly asked what the terrible things were. So Aunt
Jenny told us Grandpa was a captain of a company of men in France

during the war, and they spent hours and hours holding the Germans back from crossing an important bridge. When the war was over, Grandpa was awarded a medal for his bravery. But ever after, poor Grandpa suffered from his wounds, not just ones you could see, like the trembling in his hands, but there were wounds in his mind, too. Aunt Jenny told us that Gigi worked really hard to protect Grandpa and that we needed to be careful, too.

We asked Aunt Jenny what Uncle Jesse was like. Lovable, she said. Like Randy and Cousin Peter rolled into one. And that was the last time I remember having a conversation about Uncle Jesse, so to tell the truth, most of the time I forget he even existed. It was shocking when Randy brought him up last night.

Ivy's diary

I am kind of wishing that instead of going up to Otter Lake tomorrow, Mom and Dad could have let me stay at music camp. I miss camp so much. The master classes with Tōru Kameda were totally amazing. In about five minutes, I learned more from him than I've learned in five years from my teachers at home.

I loved learning to sail at camp so much, too. Once I was good enough, they even let me go out by myself. They knew I didn't want to compete, so they never made me race. Sometimes it just feels good to do things because I like doing them, and not because I have to prove anything to anyone else.

But tomorrow we go up to Otter Lake, and there's nothing I can do about it. I'm looking forward to seeing Gigi and Grandpa, of course, and I love Tucker and the twins, but I'm dreading seeing Tina. She just gets more obnoxious by the minute. I could hardly stand her at Thanksgiving, not that *anything* was good about that Thanksgiving.

And normally I'd be so excited to see Holly, but all Holly talks about in her letters now is boys. We always swore we'd never act stupid as we got older, but I think Holly's going to be hopeless.

It'll be strange, too, because Holly will be there without her parents. Aunt Jenny and Uncle Mike are going to be in California for almost the whole time. They told Holly she could go with them but that she'd probably be bored because they'll be teaching art history courses all day at the summer school at Berkeley. So I guess Holly thought about it, but she finally decided she couldn't possibly *not* be at Otter Lake. She said she'd spent a part of every summer of her life at the lake with Grandpa and Gigi and all the aunts and uncles and cousins—and most especially *me*! But what if she's given up this great trip to California and we don't get along?

Our cousins Peter and Miranda won't be at Otter Lake for most of the time. That's bad, because Tina is easier to take when she's with Miranda, and Peter is nice and he's funny.

4

Randy has gotten soooo serious, and I'm worried that he will be fighting with Dad the whole time, or that Mom will be nagging Sam to study math, or she'll make me go to the church dances, and also that she and Dad will be fighting in front of the rest of the family, which will be horrible.

Ever since Thanksgiving, Mom and Dad's fighting has gotten worse, and it scares me.

Oh, Otter Lake. It used to be the place where there were no troubles, and I could be happy. I want to be there and have everything be the way it used to be.

Holly

1

So I rode from Boston up to New Hampshire in Uncle Jimmy's new van, sitting in the way-back between the six-year-old twins, Tigs and Tally. I played Twenty Questions with the girls for an hour, and listened to Tucker and Tina bicker in the middle seat for another hour. Aunt Kate turned around every five minutes to tell them to be quiet until Uncle Jimmy pulled over and said he wouldn't drive anymore until they stopped.

I was so relieved when we rolled into the driveway at Otter Lake. As soon as I piled out of the van behind the twins and Tucker and Tina, I was caught up in a big hug from Gigi, and Grandpa took my suitcase, and Ivy's mom, Aunt Sandy, gave me a peck on the cheek, and then there was Ivy's brother, Sam, with a new buzz cut. He came up and punched me lightly on the arm. He'd grown like a weed, and then Ivy's oldest brother, Randy, came up and said hi. I was shocked to see him. His hair was so long, tied back in a ponytail, and he had a huge, bushy beard. Then Ivy's dad, Uncle Jake, came out of nowhere and gave me a bear hug, which surprised me, because mostly I didn't think Uncle Jake noticed me much.

"Going to miss your mother," he said.

Uncle Jake had a soft spot for Mom, maybe because she was the youngest and the only girl, but without Mom around, I planned to keep out of his way, because he had a bad temper and he scared me.

I looked around for Ivy, but she was standing back from all the commotion as if she were on this little island of shyness all by herself.

"We're going to miss your parents, but thank goodness you're here, Holly," Gigi said. She looked so safe and familiar, with her curly gray hair and her blue jeans with the cuffs rolled up at the bottom.

"It just wouldn't be the same without you," said Grandpa. "And we'll take good care of you, I promise." His face shone with excitement beneath his boating cap. Gigi often jokingly said that Grandpa loved his students when he was a history professor, but when he retired, he transferred all his love to his grandchildren.

It's going to be okay without Mom and Dad, I thought, relief welling up, and I knew I had made the right decision.

I ran over to Ivy, and we stood facing each other in the driveway. I hadn't seen her since Thanksgiving, when there was this really terrible scene at the table right after Grandpa served the turkey. Uncle Jake yelled so much at Randy that Aunt Sandy left the table in tears.

"When'd you get here?" I asked Ivy, feeling shy myself suddenly. She had grown like a weed, too, and her hair was so long I couldn't even see her pointy elf ears anymore.

"This morning." Ivy's voice was soft, and I had to lean in to hear her.

"Did you like music camp?" I asked.

"I liked sailing," said Ivy, nodding slightly. "And they had this great Japanese guy teaching a master class for the pianists—he was amazing."

I grabbed Ivy's hand. "*Uma cotcha walla,*" I said, giggling a bit. I was worried Ivy would think our secret Walla Walla language was babyish, but she said "*Uma cotcha walla*" back, and we shook hands, palms flat, then fingers curled, and then palms flat again.

Tina caught us at it. She came over, grinning, twisting one of her new pearl stud earrings around and around in her ear. "You guys are thirteen and you're still doing that?"

"So what if we are?" Ivy said, her face turning red.

"Come on, Ivy," I said. "Let's go to the Sunbird."

Ivy took off at a run, and I followed.

Too bad for Tina she wouldn't have Miranda around for most of the time we were up here this summer, but that was her problem. Ivy and I had more than a month ahead of us, even if things had been kind of awkward between us for a few seconds.

I breathed in the smell of pine needles warmed by the sun, and Otter Lake happiness expanded all through me. Halfway down the hill from the house to the lake was the Sunbird Tree. We stood in front of it, and then put out our hands to touch the Sunbird itself. No one in the family seemed to know who had carved it into the trunk of the big pine, but there it was—a circle with rays pointing out of it like a little kid's drawing of a sun, and inside the circle was a bird with outstretched wings.

We touched the Sunbird first for good luck and then chanted the Sunbird charm. *"Grant us our wish, O Sunbird Tree, and we will be grateful for eternity."*

As I closed my eyes to make a wish, I guess I felt a little embarrassed. Maybe all this chanting and wishing was like putting on a sweater you really loved, even though you knew it was too small and it didn't really fit anymore. I tried to concentrate.

Please let this time at Otter Lake with Ivy be fun.

I opened my eyes first. Ivy looked a little pinched, and she seemed to take forever over her wish. When she finally opened her eyes, I felt shy again.

"Come on, let's go down to the lake," she said.

As she took off, I ran after her. She ran like a deer, graceful and easy, and here I was, bopping along like a bunny rabbit.

Grandpa was standing on the dock next to an old wooden boat resting on sawhorses. As we joined him, he pointed to it, and I thought the trembling in his hands seemed worse.

"How would you two girls like to have your own boat to kick about in while you're here? I've been cleaning out the barn, something I've been meaning to do for years, and what do you know, this old rowboat was hiding in the back behind a stack of old boards. I sanded her down and caulked the holes, but I've left the fun of painting to the two of you. So, what do you think?"

"I'd love that!" I said, but Ivy didn't say anything. She'd written from camp saying how much she was loving learning to sail. Probably an old rowboat would be boring to her. Looking closely at the hull, I said, "It used to have stripes or something—what color was it before?"

"All the colors of the rainbow," said Grandpa. He paused, clearing his throat. "They even called her *Rainbow*. Had her out all hours of the day, exploring, fishing."

"Who did?" Ivy asked.

"Well, your father, for one, Ivy," said Grandpa quietly.

"Oh!" said Ivy, interested suddenly.

"And—well." Grandpa stopped short and then quickly looked away at something out on the lake. He had almost mentioned some other person,

I was sure of it. A shadowy image floated into my mind. I saw two boys sitting side by side in the rowboat. Uncle Jake and—it dawned on me that Uncle Jake's twin brother, Jesse, was the other boy, our uncle who had died in the war. I was amazed. Grandpa had been about to say his name out loud. Grandpa never talked about Uncle Jesse. No one ever talked about Uncle Jesse. We weren't *allowed* to.

I felt a tingling on the back of my neck. It seemed *important*, suddenly, to bring the rowboat back to life. I couldn't stop myself. I said, "Can we paint her like a rainbow again?"

"We don't have to," said Ivy quickly, frowning at me. I knew she didn't want me upsetting Grandpa.

Grandpa brought his gaze back to the boat and seemed to consider for a long minute. Then he said quietly, "You could paint her like a rainbow again. I wouldn't—" He struggled for a moment. "It will be a big project. You'll need two coats, at least."

I saw the two boys in the boat again, as clear as day. I clapped my hands. "Come on, Ivy, let's do it!" I circled the boat, excited.

"I guess," said Ivy, looking at Grandpa in a worried way.

"I'll go out and get you the marine paint and brushes," said Grandpa. "And you'll find masking tape in the boathouse if you want to start marking out the stripes."

"He almost mentioned Uncle Jesse," I said to Ivy as soon as he left.

"He didn't mean to," said Ivy. "He caught himself. I don't know if this rainbow thing is a good idea."

"It was *his* idea," I said.

"It was *your* idea."

"No, it really was his idea."

Gigi came down onto the dock. "Thought you girls might want to swim, so I—" She broke off when saw the rowboat. "Ted did say he was going to let you use the old rowboat. I didn't realize he'd already brought it down."

"Grandpa says we can paint her like she used to be painted, like a rainbow," I said.

"He *kind* of said so," said Ivy.

"He just left to go and buy us the paint," I said.

Gigi opened her mouth to say something and then closed it. She put out a hand and gently ran her fingers along the old gray wood. "She was a lovely little boat in her day. Perhaps he—well—if he's going along with it, it can't hurt. But go on, girls, put on your suits. I'm sure you'll need new ones, but last summer's will do for now."

We raced into the boathouse. Same as always, Uncle Jake's sailboat was suspended from the ceiling. He'd soon be racing it in the August Series.

"The *Ginny G* isn't here," I said, staring at the empty stall where Grandpa's old wooden motorboat, named for his mother, was usually tied up.

"Grandpa's fixing her up. She's in the barn," said Ivy.

Everything else in the boathouse seemed just the same. It even smelled the same, a sweet-sour smell of damp towels and gasoline and bat droppings—but then I felt a shiver go all through me. I'd read somewhere that ghosts could have a certain scent. *Uncle Jesse,* I thought, looking at the dust motes dancing in the shafts of sun that came in through the dusty windows. *Uncle Jesse, you're here with us.*

"I have this feeling," I said, turning to Ivy. "About Uncle Jesse. Like he's connected to the rowboat somehow. Not stored away in the barn anymore."

Ivy shook her head. "Stop it. You're giving me the creeps."

We found last summer's bathing suits in the changing lockers. Ivy squealed as she put hers on, and mine barely fit at all. It was funny, but also humiliating. We kept our T-shirts on over the bathing suits.

And then we ran out onto the dock and leaped into the lake at the same moment. When I came up to the surface, I floated on my back, soaking up the lake and the sky and the dark black-green pines. Gigi was on the dock watching over us, and then I felt the tingling on the back of my neck again. *Uncle Jesse is watching over us, too.*

The lake was so blue, and the boathouse was freshly painted bright red. The white sandy beach curled away from the dock in a big smile around the sheltered cove. I couldn't wait to be sitting on the dock again with a sketchbook, drawing and painting everything around me.

Glancing up the hill, I could just make out Otter Lake House perched up on the pine-needley knoll. Big and brown, with all its windows wide open, it was if the house were grinning and saying, *I'm sooo, sooo happy you're here again!*

And I answered back, *I'm sooo, soo happy to be here, too.*

Holly

2

By suppertime my eyes were so waterlogged the candlelight on the long table looked like starry flowers. I sat in my usual place across from Ivy, where we could make faces at each other. Gigi and Grandpa sat at either end, while the uncles and aunts and cousins sat on benches along the sides.

There was more room at the table than usual without Mom and Dad, and the British Faction wasn't up at Otter Lake yet, either. The British Faction was what we called Uncle John's family because Uncle John was married to Aunt Felicity, who was English, and even though Uncle John was American, he had an English accent, too. Mom said it was because he'd spent years in England training to be an actor. Now he was a director of his own theater company, and the accent just seemed to go with the job.

There was a gap at the table where Randy was supposed to sit. He came to supper a little late, and the moment he sat down, Uncle Jake opened his mouth to say something. I felt a little twist in my stomach, remembering Thanksgiving. Before he could say a word, Aunt Sandy snapped, "Leave him alone, Jake."

"I was just going to ask when he's going to shave," said Uncle Jake, "or get a haircut."

Almost every boy I knew at home had longish hair, but not as long as Randy's. He was going to the University of California in Berkeley, where Mom and Dad were teaching for the summer. In one of her letters, Ivy had told me he'd almost been kicked out because he was involved with student protests. It was just one of the reasons, she said, that he and Uncle Jake were having trouble getting along.

"Oh, Jake, give it a rest," said Aunt Sandy. With her bleached-blond hair piled up high, she was hands down the most glamorous of the aunts, even if her eye makeup did make her look a little like a raccoon. She had lost weight, though, or something. She looked different—tighter around her cheekbones.

"I could use your help with *Ginny G*, Randy," said Grandpa, turning to Randy. The fork Grandpa was holding was shaking like crazy and I realized the trembling in his hands was getting worse. "The rings of the engine have all seized up, so I've been trying to take it apart. I've been waiting for you to get here to put it back together."

"That's right, keep him busy so he can't stir up trouble," said Uncle Jake.

I looked up at the beams in the ceiling. Safer to look up there than at Grandpa's trembling hands or at Randy and Uncle Jake glaring at each other.

"We'll probably have to remove the heads and bore out the cylinders and put new rings and bearings on," Randy said in a fake-cheerful voice.

"Our teacher got a new ring," Tally said.

"It's a diamond ring," said Tigs. "It's really pretty."

Everyone laughed, maybe a little too loudly, but all at once, everyone began talking over everyone else.

"…church bazaar…" (Gigi to Aunt Kate.)

"…the Battle of the Bulge…" (Uncle Jimmy explaining something about World War II to Sam, who was sitting next to him.)

"…spar varnish, a couple of coats…" (Grandpa to Randy.)

I could breathe now and bring my eyes back down from the ceiling. I let all the familiar voices sink into me. Aunt Kate turned and asked me about my year at school, and I told her about playing Puck in A *Midsummer Night's Dream*.

"You've always had a flair for acting, Holly," said Aunt Kate. "There's an acting bug that runs through the Greenwood family, but Tina certainly didn't inherit it. Not that she can't be dramatic," she added, laughing. "But, honestly, Tina can only ever be Tina!"

I always thought of Uncle Jimmy's family as the "shiny" Greenwoods. Tina's and Tucker's and Tigs's and Tally's school shoes were always polished, their sneakers were never dirty, their hair was always neat and combed, their socks were always white, and their shirts stayed tucked in. Aunt Kate and Uncle Jimmy always wore matching clothes, too, like right now Uncle Jimmy was wearing a navy-blue polo shirt with green pants and Aunt Kate was wearing a green blouse tucked into navy-blue Bermuda shorts. The only sign of imperfection in the whole family was that now Tucker's bangs were a little long, and he kept twitching them out of his eyes.

In the middle of dessert, there was a lull in the conversation. Uncle Jake leaned across the table toward Ivy and said, "Your counselor told us you excelled in sailing at camp, so if we were to get you a sailboat, how about racing in the Junior Series?"

Ivy looked down at her plate. She didn't say anything, but she turned red.

"Is that a yes?"

"Don't put her on the spot at the dinner table, Jake," said Aunt Sandy.

"You don't have to, Ives," said Randy.

"She doesn't *have* to, but I would like her to," said Uncle Jake.

"I like to sail," said Ivy softly, "but I don't like to compete."

Uncle Jake frowned. "What do you mean? Aren't you spending hours and hours practicing the piano for that competition? I was thinking of getting you a sailboat for up here."

Ivy blushed even more, and Tigs said, "I know a joke. Can I tell my joke?"

Tigs told her joke and everyone laughed, and Gigi served more pie. Uncle Jake seemed to drop the whole thing, but I noticed that Ivy sat really still, not eating at all.

After supper we helped clear up and wash the dishes, and then Sam, Tucker, Tigs and Tally, and I sat at the table playing cards. Grandpa settled into his armchair by the big stone fireplace reading the newspaper, and Gigi worked on a jigsaw puzzle at a little table near him. Aunt Kate sat and knitted, and Uncle Jimmy sprawled on a couch reading a book. Tina sprawled on another couch reading magazines. Aunt Sandy stuffed herself into the little telephone closet, and we could hear her gabbing away.

"Where's Randy?" Ivy asked, looking around.

"Who cares?" asked Sam. "Sulking somewhere like always."

"What about Dad?"

Sam's and Ivy's eyes met. Sam swallowed hard. "He said he's going to put his sailboat in the water."

"By himself?"

"He likes doing stuff by himself," said Sam. His voice was kind of strained. Then he said, "You should have said yes about the sailboat, Ivy. It wouldn't hurt to try to make him happy."

"It's none of your business," Ivy snapped.

"I have one queen," I said, quickly putting down a two of spades.

"I doubt it," said Sam.

"Okay, take a look, then, if you don't believe me."

Sam turned over the cards and yelped at the two. "Take the pile, Holly-Lolly."

I scooped up the pile and then it was Sam's turn. He looked at his cards and said, "I have four kings," with a completely straight face.

"I doubt it," said Tucker, twitching the hair out of his eyes.

"Here you go, then," Sam said, smirking. He slapped four kings down in front of Tucker.

"Come play with us, Tina," said Tigs.

"I hate that game," said Tina, her nose in *Teen World*.

It wasn't long before Sam got rid of all his cards. He went and sat beside Tina and looked over her shoulder, reading bits from the magazine aloud in a funny voice.

"*Every girl has plucked daisy petals to learn about true love—No one at the hootenanny gave a hoot about me because of my oily complexion—Don't let them call you Skinny....Ask for Wate-On at your drugstore—*"

Tina slammed the magazine shut and said, "There's never any peace and quiet around here!" She flounced out of the room and then you could hear her flouncing all three stories up to the bedroom we called the Tower Room, at the top of the house.

We played a little longer, and Tucker won, which made him happy because he hardly ever won at anything. Then the twins went up to their little room on the second floor next to Aunt Kate and Uncle Jimmy's room. Sam and Tucker and I played Slapjack until Sam slapped Tucker's hand too hard. Tucker was almost in seventh grade and he still cried sometimes. He started to cry now, but then he went out to the loft over the barn where the boys slept, and Sam pulled a huge book about Winston

Churchill out of the bookshelf and started reading it. Ivy and I went up to the Tower Room.

Tina's transistor radio was on, blasting out "Mrs. Brown, You've Got a Lovely Daughter," and she was stretched out on the bottom of the bunk she shared with our cousin Miranda. Tina's head was tilted back, and she had one arm stretched up with a pen in it. She was writing on the wooden slats that supported the mattress above her head.

"What are you writing?" I asked.

"None of your beeswax," said Tina.

"That's Miranda's bed," said Ivy.

"She isn't going to be here most of the time, so I get her bed this summer," said Tina. "She said I could have it."

A minute later she went into the bathroom. Ivy and I looked at each other and then scrambled onto the bed to see what Tina had written.

Best Kissers: Rob A., Dan W., Will O.
Next Best: Brian N., Harlan W.
Bad: Johnny D.

"Poor Johnny," I giggled.

We heard the latch of the bathroom door click open and threw ourselves onto the floor, pretending to read the magazines that were scattered there.

"Nice try, guys," Tina said.

"Who's Johnny?" I asked.

"Oh, please," said Tina.

I got into my pj's, brushed my teeth, and climbed up onto the top bed of the bunk I shared with Ivy.

I lay back with my hands folded under my head. I loved being up so high. When I looked out of the Tower Room windows, I felt like I was in a giant tree house up in the tops of the pines that surrounded the house. And I loved looking at the knots in the pine board ceiling, too. There was one right over my head that looked like a rabbit with long, floppy ears. Funny thing was, if I turned my head slightly, the ears turned into the legs of a deer. It was a rabbit-deer—part Ivy, part me.

"Are you going to have the radio on the whole time we're here, Tina?" Ivy suddenly blurted out.

"I suppose you want to listen to *Beethoven*," said Tina. "My music isn't good enough for you."

"I just like it to be quiet sometimes," said Ivy.

Tina reached over and snapped off the radio. She went into the bathroom again and slammed the door.

I closed my eyes. I really didn't want to spend the whole time at Otter Lake caught in the middle of Tina and Ivy.

Ivy's diary

I'm at Otter Lake now.

I drove up from New Jersey to New Hampshire with Randy, and Sam went with Mom and Dad. I was so happy to get to ride with Randy, because in the past year I've hardly seen him at all. He didn't come up to Otter Lake last summer because he went down to Mississippi to do some civil rights stuff, and then he went straight back to college after he was finished. All he did was fight with Dad at Thanksgiving, and he didn't come home at all for Christmas. Ever since he went away to college he seems so different and hard to talk to.

"After last summer, it's going to be difficult for me to be at Otter Lake," he said as he was driving. "I'm only coming because Gigi and Grandpa asked me to. And," he added, "it's nice spending time with you, Ivy."

That made me happy and also made it easier for me to ask him questions.

"What was it like last summer?" I asked. "I don't even really know what you were doing down in Mississippi."

"Hard to explain," he said.

"Mom was worried the whole time you were down there because she kept hearing that people were getting hurt. How come people were getting hurt?"

"You don't want to know," he said.

And I said, "I do want to know."

So Randy actually started talking then, and he pretty much talked the rest of the ride up. I don't know if I can remember everything he said, but I'm going to try. He told me he went there to register Negroes to vote in Mississippi. I asked him why he would have to do that, and he said it was because Mississippi had the lowest percentage of Negroes registered to vote in the entire country. He said the white population there was making it really difficult for them to vote. Like they made them pay a tax if they tried to register, or made them take some complicated test, or sometimes they even stopped them from registering at gunpoint.

"At gunpoint?" I asked, shocked.

"Yes," Randy said.

"I didn't know it was that bad," I said.

"It was worse than anything you might imagine," he said. "I was pretty innocent myself before I went down there. We had a training session in Ohio before we got to Mississippi. The first thing we learned was that three activists had been missing for sixteen hours and they were probably dead. I couldn't believe it—that murders had already taken place. I tell you, Ivy, I was scared out of my mind. But then this woman got up on the stage, and she started singing 'Go Tell It on the Mountain,' and everyone was singing and rocking and swaying with their arms around each other, and that's when I learned how when you sing with a whole bunch of other people, you can become less afraid."

Randy told me how in that training session he was taught nonviolent resistance. To fall on the ground, to roll up in a ball, to cover his neck and hands, so if he got hit with billy clubs, it would do less damage.

"With billy clubs?" I asked. The whole idea of it was making me feel sick.

"Billy clubs were the least of it. Try fire hoses. Try bullets."

"But why?" I asked.

"Many of the white people down there were very angry at us," Randy said. "They said we were interfering. That what went on in their home state was none of our business."

Randy was quiet for a minute, and I guess he was just remembering stuff. Then he went on. "I was with a group that went to a town called Canton. It was about ten miles from Jackson, and there were more Negroes than whites living there, but when we arrived, the white folks came up to us and spat on us and called us names and cursed and threatened us. They kept yelling and telling us to go home."

Randy told me that while he was down south he lived with a family of sharecroppers. There was no mail delivery there. No plumbing. No running water. The family's job was picking cotton. Randy tried picking cotton to see what it was like. He had to quit after only an hour. He said it tore up his hands and he just couldn't do it anymore. He said the sacks they dragged around were so heavy he could hardly lift them.

"That's so terrible," I said.

Randy told me that over a thousand people went down to Mississippi to help. It made the white people so mad, they bombed and burned the churches that were trying to help the Negroes. Four people were killed. Eighty people were beaten.

I asked him if he had been beaten, and he said yes.

He said that one day he was in a car driving to a church with two other college students when they noticed a pickup truck following them. The truck forced them off the road and these guys came out shouting "Nigger lovers!" They beat Randy up and kicked him down a bank, and all these people were watching from their porches and lawns and didn't do anything.

Now I really felt sick to my stomach.

"Dad should know about this," I said.

Randy said, "I can't talk to Dad. I wish I could. I mean, I think his own experiences in the war must have been terrible, but he won't talk about them, so I'll never really know what happened to him. Any more than we'll ever know what really happened to Uncle Jesse. And I'm guessing Dad would say I never should have put myself in the middle of something like the civil rights movement. He'd say what happened to me was my own fault."

I said, "But, Randy, you were so *brave*. Mom and Dad ought to know how brave you were."

"I wasn't brave," he said. "I was scared the whole time."

I don't know what to do with everything Randy told me. I've always looked up to him, but now I look up to him even more.

What I really, really want to do is ask him if he thinks Mom and Dad are going to get a divorce, because that's what I'm beginning to think is going to happen. I want to ask him, but I'm afraid of what he might say.

Okay, I just told Tina to turn down the radio. Her stupid music was beginning to get to me. Oh, brother. Is this how it's going to be the whole time we're here?

Holly

3

In the morning, Ivy and I ran down to the dock as soon as breakfast was over. The twins came down with Aunt Kate, and they went over to the beach. Tina brought down her radio and a stack of magazines. She settled into a deck chair in her bikini with suntan lotion slathered all over her. The boys came down to look at the boat.

"Where'd it come from, anyway? The rowboat?" Randy asked.

"It was Dad's," said Ivy.

"And Uncle Jesse's," I said.

"How do you know that?" asked Sam.

"Grandpa told us the rowboat belonged to your dad, and then he *almost* said, 'and Uncle Jesse.'"

"Whoa," said Randy. "That's a first."

"Uncle Jesse died in the war, right?" Tina asked. She was sitting up now, looking thoughtful.

"No," said Sam. He ran a hand across his buzzed head. Everyone was staring at him. "That's what they all say, but that's not how he died."

Tina gave him a dirty look. "Well, if you know something, spit it out!"

"I overheard Uncle John and Uncle Jimmy talking last Easter, and—I don't know if I should tell you."

I could see that Sam was bursting to tell us what he knew. Keeping a secret since April—it must have been killing him. He finally hunched his shoulders and swallowed hard, and the Adam's apple in his skinny throat bounced. "Okay, I'm not totally sure," he said, "but it sounded like one day Dad and Jesse were out in the *Ginny G*. They were fooling around, going around in circles, going really fast, and Jesse fell out, and the— and the motorboat ran over him—" Sam closed his mouth and just stood there.

There was complete silence on the dock.

"It would explain why they don't like talking about Uncle Jesse," said Randy slowly. "And it would explain why Dad got so angry when I brought him up the other night. I wish I'd known about this before, Sam." He looked at Sam accusingly.

Sam looked down at his sneakers. "It's not like you're that easy to tell things to."

There was silence on the dock again. Then Randy said, "Tucker and Sam, we should go up to the barn. Grandpa will be waiting for us."

"I don't want to work on the motorboat anymore," said Tucker. His eyes were full of tears. This time I didn't blame him. I felt like crying myself.

"Come on, Tuck," said Randy, clapping a hand on his shoulder. "Grandpa needs your help."

"I'd rather work on the rowboat," said Tucker.

"You know what? It's probably not even true," Tina snapped. "Don't you think we'd know it if that was what happened?"

Sam glared at her. "I wish I'd never opened my big mouth."

"Are you going to help Ivy and Holly work on the rowboat, Tina?" Randy asked.

"No, I'm working on my tan," said Tina, and she lay back down.

The radio blared, "Love, love me do," and as the boys drifted up the hill to the barn, Ivy and I started marking off the stripes with the masking tape Grandpa had set out for us. To make myself feel better, I yelled along with the radio. Ivy made a face. She wanted me not to like popular music. Me, I liked both kinds of music, and there wasn't anything she could do about it.

"Be more careful," Ivy said to me after a while. The tape I was trying to put down kept wrinkling. "This was Dad's boat, and he hates people to be sloppy."

"It wasn't just his—it was Uncle Jesse's boat, too," I reminded her. I stopped working for a moment and looked around. "It's strange thinking about him. I mean, he was a boy once, standing on this dock painting this boat, and now he doesn't exist anymore."

I had seen a photo of Uncle Jake when he was a boy. He was skinny, with a lot of black hair. I tried to remember what Uncle Jesse had looked like in a photograph Ivy and I had found of him. Gigi had taken it from us so quickly I couldn't remember it at all. I didn't even know if Jake and Jesse had been identical twins.

Speaking of twins, Tigs and Tally suddenly started laughing really loudly. Ivy and I looked over at them across the cove where they were making sand castles. Gigi was back from church and had joined Aunt Kate. They were both sitting on the beach in beach chairs, reading and chatting with each other.

Mom was usually there with them. She always said the five weeks at Otter Lake was such a relaxing time for the aunts. They got to be together, helping each other with the cooking and each other's kids, while the uncles mostly came and went on the weekends because they had their jobs—all of them except for Uncle Jake, who was able to take most of August off.

Tigs and Tally left their castles and paddled around in the water.

"Remember when we had underwater tea parties?" I asked Ivy.

"I wish we were Tigs and Tally's age again," she said with a sigh. "Remember how we didn't even wear bathing suits? We just wore shorts."

"Your mom and Aunt Kate are taking you and me and Tina to get new bathing suits tomorrow."

Ivy made a face. "Shopping with Mom. Equals torture."

I sighed. "I doubt if Aunt Kate will be much better. I'm sure she won't like anything I pick out." And I wished I'd gone shopping with Mom before coming up here.

"You know what I just realized?" Ivy asked suddenly. "My mom never sits on the beach with the others. I don't see why she can't just fit in." Her voice trembled slightly. "She hates having to spend every summer vacation here. It's one of the things she and Dad fight about." She kept her head down and rubbed a finger over a section of tape again and again.

"Fighting stinks," I said, thinking about Aunt Sandy and Uncle Jake, and then I felt scared suddenly, as if I were swimming in dark, deep water where I couldn't see the bottom. I wanted to stay up on the surface of things. "It's worse than stinks," I blurted out. "Like how the outhouse smells at the mountain."

Ivy's head shot up and her blue eyes blazed at me. "You know what, Holly? You turn everything into a stupid joke." She grabbed up a roll of masking tape and started picking furiously at it.

"I'm sorry, Ivy—I know that was really dumb." I reached out and took the roll from her so she had to look at me. "I mean it. I'm sorry."

"Okay," she said, but looked quickly away again.

We worked on marking out stripes all morning, and then Gigi and Aunt Kate went up to the house to make lunch, and the twins came over to the dock. Tina yelled at them for dripping water on her. And then everything stopped as Gigi and Aunt Kate brought down baskets of sandwiches and lemonade. Grandpa and Uncle Jimmy and the boys came down for lunch, too. I checked out Uncle Jimmy's feet. Yup. Just like always when he was at Otter Lake, he was wearing shiny loafers but no socks. That was *relaxed* for him.

"Where are Mom and Dad?" asked Sam, looking around.

"Jake and Sandy have gone off for the afternoon," said Aunt Kate. Her green hairband matched her green shorts and her green canvas shoes and Uncle Jimmy's green polo shirt. "Mysterious errand. Jake was all spiffed up, wearing a suit. Sandy looked like she was going to dine out in New York."

Randy and Sam and Ivy looked at each other.

"No idea," said Randy with a shrug.

After lunch, Grandpa said, "Keep the paint between the lines. Only dip the brush halfway in, like this." He demonstrated. "If you dunk the brush all the way into the can, the paint will glop on too thickly and make a mess. And move the boat out of the sun, otherwise the paint will blister."

The radio was blaring "(I Can't Get No) Satisfaction." As we painted, bugs and pine needles kept drifting into the wet paint. After a while, my back ached from all the bending over.

"Ugh," I said. I straightened up and used the inside of my elbow to push the hair out of my eyes.

Tucker wandered down from working on the motorboat and jumped into the lake. He came up looking so happy, we decided to go in, too. Even Tina joined us. We swam out to the little floating dock anchored a short distance from the beach and then played the Last One Standing game. Tucker was the best at knocking people off, and Tina screamed so loudly she made my ears hurt.

When we came back in, Tucker begged us to let him help paint. Ivy didn't want him to, but I felt sorry for him. He so often had to do chores with the older boys when he just wanted to do fun things with us. He turned out to be surprisingly careful. By late afternoon, we had actually put on the first coat.

"Hot tamales," said Tucker, standing back and admiring the boat, "it's beautiful."

"*She*," Tina said from her sunbathing position on the dock. "Boats are shes."

Sam and Randy came down the hill for a swim. After they got out of the water, Sam stood on the dock in front of *Rainbow*. "Man, dig that boat. What gave you the idea of painting it like a rainbow?"

"Boats are shes," Tina said again, twirling an earring.

"Grandpa said that's how Dad painted her," said Ivy.

"That's so cool," said Randy. He walked all around the boat, but then he stood stock-still. "By the way, does Dad know you're doing this?"

Ivy and I looked at each other.

"I don't know," said Ivy.

Randy rolled his eyes, and then he said, "Well, hold on to your hats, because here he comes."

Uncle Jake, looking out of place in a suit and tie, was making his way down the steps to the dock. He stopped in front of the rowboat and stared. Then he said, "Who the devil gave you permission to use this boat and paint it like this?"

We all of us froze into statues.

"Didn't you hear me?" he bellowed. "Whose idea was this?"

Ivy seemed to shrink into the shadows. My chest tightened. But suddenly I wasn't hearing his yelling—I was seeing a boy. I couldn't see his face clearly, but he was saying, "I'm glad you're painting the rowboat like a rainbow again."

I took a deep breath and stood up straight. I turned my hands into fists and faced Uncle Jake. "Grandpa gave us the boat, and he said we could paint her the way she used to be. He said the rowboat was yours and—and—and—" Everyone on the dock flinched, and I stopped myself just in time from saying Jesse's name out loud. I was shaking so much even my voice was wobbly. "It's not hurting anything for us to have it, I mean *her*, and I think she's beautiful."

Uncle Jake pulled his face into a ferocious scowl. I bit my lips to stop my tears. I did *not* want to cry in front of Uncle Jake.

"We worked really hard to do it right," I added faintly. "We used masking tape and everything."

Uncle Jake started circling the boat. The boy I had pictured in my mind wasn't there anymore, and I no longer felt as brave as I had before.

Finally Uncle Jake stood still and sighed. Then he sighed again. And then he said, "You've done a classy job. Couldn't have done better myself." He thumped my shoulder with his big bear paw of a hand. "Tell you what—first bass you catch from this rowboat, Holly, I'll clean it and show you how to cook it up." And then he lumbered back up the hill.

As soon as he was out of sight, Sam said, "Wow, Holly. If I'd spoken up to Dad like that, he would have grounded me for a year."

I sat down on the dock, trying to get my legs to stop shaking. "I sort of had—I thought of Uncle Jesse—I wanted to stick up for him."

Tina was rolling and unrolling a strand of hair between her fingers. "I hate to say this, you guys," she said, "but your dad kind of scares me. I'm glad he's not my dad."

Sam kicked one of Tina's magazines. "Thanks, Tina, you're a big help."

Ivy's diary

Sunday, July 25, 1965

Stupid radio is on.

I know where Mom and Dad went today. They're looking at boarding schools for Sam and me. I saw all the brochures for the schools by Mom's bedside table. It's because they're planning on splitting up and they need to find a place to stick us so they don't have to worry about us.

Sam's story about Uncle Jesse and the motorboat is awful, and I wish I'd never heard it.

Dad was so scary when he saw the rowboat. And the way Holly stood up to him surprised me. I couldn't believe how Dad just sort of stopped being mad.

Holly and I went to the bog after that. It's where we go when something really upsetting happens, like when Gigi's cocker spaniel died, or when Sam nearly cut off his finger with a knife and he had to go to the hospital. It's so quiet and peaceful in the bog, it always makes us feel better.

I said, "Let's make a vow never to change."

"What do you mean?" Holly asked.

"I just feel like everything's changing," I said. "Like Sam and Tina aren't as much fun as they used to be, and Randy is so serious all the time, and—" *And he was beaten up last summer and no one even knows about it, and I'm scared my parents are going to get a divorce*—but I didn't think I could say any of those things to Holly. She couldn't even handle me talking about them fighting.

"Okay," she said. "If we're going to make a vow, we have to make a sacrifice."

She went over to a bush and picked two blueberries and gave me one. Then we knelt at the edge of the bog and she put out her hand and plopped her berry into the cupped leaves of a pitcher plant. I plopped in mine. The two blue knobs floated side by side.

28

Holly said, "If the pitcher plant gags on the berry, maybe a frog could come and do mouth-to-mouth."

"Stop trying to be funny," I said. "You used to be able to take things seriously. What we have to do now is make our vow. Like this. I, Ivy Pierce Greenwood, solemnly vow never to change."

"Okay, I, Hollis Greenwood Swanson, vow never to change," said Holly in an overdramatic voice. She is such a pain sometimes.

And then I shivered, thinking of Uncle Jesse. Only dead people didn't change. The bog seemed too quiet. I jumped up, nearly making Holly lose her balance, and I started running. I ran until we came out onto the dirt road, where huge ferns were growing along the side. Holly was right behind me.

"Whoa, what happened to you?" she asked.

"I got spooked in there," I said.

I picked two fern fronds and began flapping them.

"I'm flying!" I shouted, laughing my head off and feeling a little crazy.

Holly wrenched two more ferns from their stems. We ran, flapping the fern wings all the way back to the house.

Two months until the competition. I'm trying to practice on the old piano here but it's so terrible. Some of the keys stick, and it hasn't been tuned in about a hundred years. At camp, Tōru told me my playing should be more colorful. I don't know how to make it more colorful. I should be studying with him right now, or at least with someone like him.

Holly
4

Ivy and I painted *Rainbow* sky blue on the inside. And finally, finally, after two coats and three days of drying, we put her in the water. Her stripes made the most beautiful reflection in the water, but then she began leaking like crazy.

As we stood on the dock watching the water come in, Grandpa laughed and said, "It's all right. She just has to sit in the lake for a few days, and her old seams will swell up nice and tight."

A few days! I could hardly wait that long. But I could hear Mom's voice in my ears loud and clear, telling me not to be so impatient. *Why not make a drawing of* Rainbow *while you're waiting?* I heard her say. And it was true. I hadn't done any sketching since I'd gotten to Otter Lake.

I ran up the hill and then along the trail to the little cabin we called the studio. It was about a five-minute walk from the house, set back in the woods, but one side was all windows, with a view out to the lake.

Just as I pulled open the door and stepped inside, a long dark rope dropped from one of the beams above me. I screamed and screamed, and then I screamed again as a snake slipped down my shoulder, onto the floor, and out the door.

I stood there shaking like a leaf. My heart was racing a mile a minute. And then I burst out laughing at the racket I had just made. No one could have heard me, but if they had, they'd have thought for sure I'd almost been murdered.

I walked over and picked up a canvas the snake had knocked down onto the floor. It was of a rowboat with rainbow stripes, the colors reflecting in the water, and two boys were sitting in the middle, rowing side by side. It was so much like what I'd pictured when Grandpa first talked about *Rainbow*, I felt dizzy for a moment.

I recognized Gigi's dabby painting style, and sure enough, there in the corner was Gigi's G and the date, 1935. Sometimes Gigi wrote little notes on the backs of her paintings, describing the weather or the circumstances, so I turned it over. No notes, but tucked into a corner of the frame was a large envelope. I pulled it out. *Mrs. Greenwood* was printed on the front in large, round handwriting.

I looked around. No one was here to tell me it wasn't addressed to me or that it wasn't any of my business. I sat down in an old chair with the painting and the envelope resting on my knees. The envelope wasn't sealed. I opened it and fished out a small painting. It was of a pine tree growing on the shore of a lake.

Not so long ago, Mom and Dad had taken me to an exhibition of Japanese art, and this painting reminded me of what we had looked at. A light wash for the background. Tiny brushstrokes for the pine needles. A smudge here and there for the bark. In the corner there were what I thought were Japanese characters.

On the other side there was a note in that same round handwriting.

September, 1941

Dear Mrs. Greenwood-san,

    I am sitting in the dorm so overwhelmed that you wrote to me a letter saying not to worry about anything that has happened. I am very sad not to be with you anymore. Any sorrow I brought to your family, believe me, I am more sorry than anyone. I think often of the sun on the beautiful lake, the wind in trees. How much I love the woods on the hill behind the house. But most often, I think of the good times, many good laughters with my American family. I shall never forget you, and I always pray you do not think too badly of me, no matter what has happened.

                Much true happiness for very kind heart.
                From your friend,
                Kiyoshi

Kiyoshi. I had never heard the name before. And what was the "sorrow?" What had happened?

I got up and put the painting of *Rainbow* on the shelf with the other paintings by Gigi and Mom and me. Facing out. Front and center. And then I wondered if that was the right thing to do. I'd spent many hours here in the studio and had never seen the painting before. It had been living up on that beam because someone had put it there. I couldn't leave it on the shelf. What if Gigi came out here and saw it and got really upset?

I tucked the painting back in the envelope and the envelope back in the frame. Then I climbed up on the old chair and set the painting back on the beam.

I grabbed up a soft pencil and watercolor set and an old sketchbook of Mom's from a pile of other old sketchbooks. A few of her charcoal sketches were in it, but mostly the pages were blank. Seeing her familiar style of drawing made me miss her. I wondered if she knew who Kiyoshi was and what the "sorrow" was.

Down at the lake, I sat on the dock and started a sketch of *Rainbow* on a clean white page. Instead of putting two boys in her, I put in Ivy and me.

Ivy came down and sat beside me. She wrapped her arms around her knees and pulled herself into a tight ball.

"You okay, Ivy?"

"Mom and Dad just had another big fight."

I'd been about to tell her what I'd found in the studio. Instead I said, "I'm really sorry, Ivy."

She put her head down on her knees, and I kept drawing, wishing I knew the right words to say to her.

Rainbow stopped taking on water, and Grandpa gave us rowing lessons. I went first, by myself, and then Ivy had a turn. Ivy caught on faster than I did. She always learned things quickly, but then I had another turn, and Grandpa was really patient, and when I finally got the hang of it, he beamed at me as if I'd just climbed Mount Everest. Mom said Grandpa's students had adored him because he was such a good teacher, and I could believe it.

When he thought we had a good grasp of things, Grandpa let both of us get into *Rainbow*. He made sure we had life cushions and gave us an extra oar, in case we lost one overboard, and let us go free. "You can also row side by side, you know, each taking an oar. Sometimes the boys rowed all the way to the islands just like that." He caught himself and closed his mouth.

Gigi was standing beside him. She linked an arm through his. I heard her say, "I'm glad *Rainbow* is in the water again."

And I thought about the painting she had done of *Rainbow* in 1935. I wondered if the painting was as vivid in her mind as it was in mine.

The next morning, the minute I woke up I saw the sky. It was clear and blue. I hung my head down over the top bunk. "Hey, Ivy, let's row out to the islands today."

"After I practice," she said. "I'm falling behind."

After breakfast Ivy went and practiced on the old piano in the room off the living room. Her music filled the house. I listened with awe. I didn't know how she could memorize so many notes, but we didn't get out on the lake until after lunch.

But finally, we were sitting in *Rainbow* side by side, each of us pulling on an oar.

There was a brisk breeze blowing, so at first we kept close to the shore, and after a while we came to what had been named Secret Cove by Mom and my uncles a million years ago. A stream bubbled down into the cove, and a carpet of forget-me-nots grew on the banks. Once we were in the cove, I moved back to the stern and stretched out.

"You're covered with all these leaf shadows," said Ivy. "It makes you look like you're in one of Gigi's paintings."

Ivy was covered with shadows, too. "I went into the studio to get a sketchbook, and a snake knocked a painting down from one of the beams. I nearly had a heart attack," I said. "But anyhow, it was a painting Gigi did of *Rainbow*. Your dad and Jesse are in it. I'd never seen it before. I think it was stuck up on that beam on purpose."

"Because Jesse was in it?" I nodded, and Ivy stuck her chin in the air. "So don't go running off and telling Gigi you found it."

Her tone of voice made me not want to tell her about Kiyoshi. She'd be mad at me, anyhow, for opening an envelope that wasn't addressed to me.

"Come on, let's go to the islands now," I said.

I moved into the middle of the boat again, and we backed out of the cove using little, shallow strokes. The wind was picking up, but it was blowing in our favor, and we barely had to row.

The islands were two pancakes hitched together by a rough bridge. The smaller island was named Hermit's Haven because of the half-fallen-down shelter on it. The other was called Big Tree because one humongous pine tree grew in the middle of it. Ivy and I pulled *Rainbow* up onto the little beach on Hermit's Haven.

"Want to go swimming?" Ivy asked. "Last one in is a rotten egg."

We had so much fun swimming in and around the big rocks. Afterward, we checked out the hermit's shelter.

"Do you think a hermit really lived here?" I asked, looking around.

"I would," said Ivy. "I'd stick a piano in here and be set for life."

"Except you'd have to rebuild the shelter." I sat down on one of the beams that had fallen down. It was covered with names and initials and hearts that people had carved into it. "Do you like having to practice all the time?" I asked.

"Sometimes it's hard to get started," Ivy said, "but then, once I'm into it, I don't think about anything else."

I studied her for a minute. "Are your parents *making* you go out for this competition?"

Ivy made a face. "Kind of."

"What do you mean, kind of?"

Ivy frowned. "Competing makes all the practicing I do socially acceptable to Mom. Otherwise, she'd make me go to parties and stuff."

I was about to say parties and stuff were fun, but then a carving on the edge of the beam near my left foot caught my eye. "Hey, Ivy!" I knelt down to take a closer look. "Someone came here and carved a Sunbird on this beam! I never noticed it before."

Ivy crouched down to look, too. "It's exactly like the one on our tree. It looks old and faded, too, like it's been here for a while." She traced it with her fingers. "We don't even know who carved the Sunbird at home, do we? Isn't it strange no one seems to know or remember?"

I felt a shiver go right through me. "It was Uncle Jesse," I said. "That's why they say they can't remember."

"Yeah," said Ivy quietly.

Holly

5

We left the shelter and crossed over to the other island on the bridge and headed for the big tree. Ivy and I always climbed it when we came out to the islands. We pulled ourselves up as high as we dared and then braced ourselves against the trunk.

"There's our dock," said Ivy, pointing.

The dock was a tiny splinter of gray. The house was hidden in a band of evergreens, with another very tall pine tree standing guard at the top. There was a bare patch in the woods where Grandpa and Gigi were clearing a lot for the retirement house they were building. Mount Wigan rose up at the farthest end. The day was so clear I could make out individual trees on its ridges. A gust of wind shook the top of the tree.

"It's getting windier," I said.

"There's a sailboat!" Ivy said, pointing down at the lake now. "I bet Dad's out."

Two motorboats sped out of a cove, side by side.

"Grandpa will be launching the *Ginny G* pretty soon," I said. "I guess they've almost got her fixed up now."

I pictured the motorboat out on the lake, her varnished deck gleaming in the sunlight. I could see her turning and the bow slapping down on her own wake, but instead of Grandpa in the boat, or Randy, I saw two boys in her, yelling and shouting and laughing. They were turning in tighter and tighter circles, and then suddenly one of the boys was flung sideways, but the boat kept turning.

I had to fight a sick feeling rising in my stomach.

"I kind of wish—I kind of wish Sam hadn't told us that story about Jesse and the *Ginny* G," I said.

"I know," said Ivy.

A gust of wind rattled the top branches again.

"We should be getting back," I said. "The wind has really come up."

We climbed down and returned to Hermit's Haven. We pushed

Rainbow off the beach and finally managed to scramble into her, even though she was bouncing around like crazy. We sat side by side again, but *Rainbow* kept lurching and dipping, and Ivy almost lost an oar.

"It will work better if you row by yourself," said Ivy.

"You want *me* to row?"

"I can't afford to mess up my hands right now," she said, moving to the stern.

I felt a surge of panic. Then I thought, *I'm a good swimmer.* There was nothing to be afraid of, and we had life cushions in the boat with us. I shifted my weight so I was sitting smack in the middle of the thwart and gripped the oars and began pulling as hard as I could, trying to keep a steady course.

Deciding not to look over my shoulder until I'd rowed twenty strokes, I started to count. *One, two, three…* Big puffy clouds raced overhead, their shadows sweeping over us.

Eighteen, nineteen, twenty… I turned around. We were making progress. A motorboat zoomed by, and *Rainbow* bounced and tilted sideways in the wake. Ivy and I squealed as we took on water.

One, two, three… I counted again, pulling extra hard with my port oar to keep a steady course.

I don't know how many times I counted up to twenty, but finally we were in close to shore, and with twenty more strokes, we were into Secret Cove. I lay back, sweating. My shoulders were aching.

"Good job, Hol," said Ivy. "We made it."

"Yeah, but we still have a long way to get back." My heart sank as the wind came roaring into the cove, making *Rainbow* bang against the bank. The palms of my hands were one big blister. I could not *imagine* rowing the rest of the way home.

"There you are," said a voice. It came from a shadowy figure standing next to a tree on the bank.

My entire skull pricked as for one awful moment I thought I was seeing Uncle Jesse's ghost.

"Dad!" Ivy's eyes were huge as Uncle Jake made his way down the bank toward us. "We thought you were out sailing!"

Uncle Jake shook his head. A pair of binoculars was slung around his neck. "No," he said. "My boat's not quite ready for this weather. Will

Brown is out there by himself, and I'm telling you, that boy knows what he's doing! Anyway, I noticed you two had gone off in the rowboat. Figured you could use some help."

He squatted at the edge of the bank and reached out to pull us in. I scrambled into the stern to get out of his way as he climbed in. He sat in the middle and began rowing with quick, sure, short strokes. His arms were like tree trunks. He was so solid and real—and alive.

As soon as we were out of the cove, Uncle Jake said, "All right, Holly, you and I are going to change places. I'm going to teach you how to feather. Come on, hurry up. You move first." He shipped the oars.

"What?" I said, not quite believing what I'd heard.

"Come on," he barked.

I moved forward while Uncle Jake swung back to the stern and sat next to Ivy. I winced as my blisters met the grips of the oars again, but I had to start rowing quickly. We were being blown downwind like a piece of fluff.

After watching me row a few strokes, Uncle Jake leaned forward and grabbed my wrists. "Bend your wrists on the return stroke, like this. That way you'll turn the blades flat and there will be less resistance to the wind."

I rowed like that for a while. Feathering did seem to make a difference.

Uncle Jake sat back and rested his elbows on his knees. "Looks like you've been rowing all your life," he said.

I felt really proud. Uncle Jake was actually praising me. I glanced at Ivy. Her face was a blank. She didn't ask to row, and Uncle Jake didn't ask her to.

"I'll take over now, if you don't mind," he said after a while. We switched again, and Uncle Jake stretched his legs out in front of him, pulling the oars with wide, sweeping strokes. "Never thought I'd be doing this again," he said with a huge grin, and I thought I could see, just for a second, what kind of boy he had been. And just for a second, I imagined I saw his twin sitting beside him.

By the time the dock came in sight, the wind was dying down.

"Hey, look," I said, pointing. An animal with a dark head was swimming a little way out from the shore.

"Otter," said Uncle Jake. He stopped rowing a moment, and we watched. The little head strained forward as it swam, leaving a V-shaped wake. "Lake used to be filled with otters," he said. "In the old days before all the motorboats. And the otters used to be so trusting, they would actually swim with you. Then when motorboats came into vogue, there were folks who thought it was fun to chase the otters."

"That's terrible," I said.

Uncle Jake scowled and started rowing again with short, jerky movements. "Used to be more rowboats and canoes and sailboats in the old days. A system of boats would go from house to house delivering mail and groceries. Sometimes we would row this very boat down to the end of the lake and climb up the hill to Hutchings' and get ice cream or penny candy."

"When you say *we*, do you mean you and Uncle Jesse?"

The name slipped out, just like that. It had been on the tip of my tongue for so long I just couldn't hold it in my mouth anymore. Uncle Jake's face flushed up, and he stopped rowing again. My heart began to race, and Ivy was looking at me with wide, terrified eyes.

"I mean all of us." His words came out one by one, slowly, heavily, as if he were spitting stones.

"I think I would have liked it back then," I said, panicky, trying to cover up.

Uncle Jake scowled, but after gripping the oars hard and rowing a few brisk strokes, he sort of grunted and said, "You're an old-fashioned girl, Holly, and a rough-and-ready one, too, I'm thinking. Not worried about getting your hands messed up." He glanced at Ivy. Two red spots burned in her cheeks. Uncle Jake must have been standing on the shore watching us through his binoculars as we made our way back across the lake from the islands. He'd seen that I had done all the rowing.

"Okay, we're coming into the dock, get ready to fend off," he said, shipping the oars. "Next time *you* can do the rowing, Ivy. I'll buy you some gloves."

Uncle Jake hauled himself out of *Rainbow*, tied her up, and walked away without another word.

"You're lucky, Holly," Ivy burst out. "You don't have to be one kind of girl for your mother and the opposite kind for your father. And no one expects you to be good at anything." She started climbing out of the rowboat.

"Hold on just a minute, Ivy Greenwood." I grabbed on to the back of her shirt and made her sit down again. "Before you go storming off, are you saying I'm not good at anything?"

"I didn't mean it the way it sounded," she said. "It's just that Dad wasn't very nice to me."

"Yeah," I said, rubbing the blisters on my hand. "I'm sorry."

"And I don't see how come you can bring up Uncle Jesse and not have Dad get mad at you."

"Uncle Jesse is watching over me," I said.

"*What?* Are you crazy?"

"I'm going up the hill."

I climbed out of the boat, leaving Ivy sitting there, and stomped up the hill. Near the top, it occurred to me that Uncle Jake had been mean to Ivy, so she had turned around and had been mean to me. It was like a game of tag. You got tagged, and then you went and tagged the next person. I saw Tucker coming my way.

"Want to play badminton?" he asked. "I'm tired of working on the motorboat all day. I want to do something fun."

The *last* thing I wanted to do was hold a badminton racket in my blistery hand. But I said yes.

Holly

6

It was Sunday, and Randy and I went to church with Gigi. The sermon was about what it means to be a good friend to someone. The minister said a true friend is someone who says, "To the best of my ability, as we ride the storms of life together in this little boat, I will be here again and again for you."

I understood that he didn't mean a real boat, but all I could picture was Ivy and me coming back from the islands in *Rainbow*. It seemed to me that ever since that day we'd been more like prickly friends than true friends, and it was bothering me. Was it my fault or hers?

After the service, we went downstairs to the coffee hour. Randy and I were hanging out by the doughnuts. I felt tongue-tied around him. All the things Randy liked to talk about—Vietnam, civil rights, cylinders, pistons—they weren't really things I knew much about.

But then a bunch of old ladies noticed us and they came over and said, "My, Holly, how you've grown." And an old lady named Mrs. McCloskey came up to Randy and said, "If you didn't have all that hair, you would be the spitting image of Jesse Greenwood."

Randy said, politely, "I hope that's a good thing."

Mrs. McCloskey said, not so politely, "I just hope you don't have funny notions like he did."

"What funny notions?" Randy started to ask. I could see he was getting hot under the collar, but Gigi came over just then and said we ought to be getting home.

I climbed into the back of Gigi's old woodie station wagon while Gigi sat in the front beside Randy, who was driving.

Gigi said, "Well, I don't know what possessed you to come with us today, Randy, but I sure do love your company." She turned quickly around to look at me. "I don't want you to think I don't appreciate you, too, Holly—it's just that I never expected to see Randy in church."

"I like spending time with you, Gigi," said Randy, "but truthfully, I wanted to see what the minister here would say. The churches are playing a big part in the civil rights movement. They were the ones who set up the Freedom Schools last summer when I was down south, teaching reading skills to folks so they could register to vote. And a lot of churches here in the north are beginning to speak up for civil rights, too, as well as speak out against the war. But not in a little hick town in New Hampshire, I guess."

"You need to be careful, Randy," said Gigi. "A lot of folks who live around here lost sons in Korea, and in the last big war, and in the war before that. Honestly, I wish you wouldn't go out of your way to bash heads with people about it. I tell you this plainly—draft dodging is a very sensitive topic."

Randy made a sort of grunting noise. "Draft dodging—is that what you call it? I call it conscientious objection."

Gigi was very quiet, and Randy glanced over at her and then thumped a hand on the steering wheel. "I'm not against all war, Gigi. I would have fought against Hitler. That was a war worth fighting—not like the one they're fighting now."

"Not everyone thought that war was worth fighting," said Gigi. Her voice was wobbly and difficult to hear. I had to lean way forward to catch what she was saying. "Some people believed in their heart of hearts that it was wrong to kill others no matter what. Even with Hitler and all he was doing. Don't think you're so original, Randy." She suddenly raised her voice, beginning to sound mad. "There have always been people who don't believe in going to war."

"I don't think I'm—" Randy started to say, but Gigi interrupted him.

"And those people are considered traitors and cowards. Is that how you want people to view you, Randy? And do you want to go to prison, or—I don't know if they have them anymore—one of those CPS camps?"

"What sort of camp?" Randy was looking over at Gigi.

"CPS stands for Civilian Public Service," she said. "It was intended to be a way for the COs—that's the conscientious objectors—to serve the country honorably. Because in the First War, conscientious objectors were imprisoned and beaten and treated terribly. So when the next war came along, they created camps where men who didn't want to fight could go and do work of national importance." Gigi sighed. "National importance!

In my opinion, those camps were created to keep conscientious objectors out of sight because it was considered shameful not to go and be a soldier."

Randy looked long and hard at Gigi again. "How do you know so much about this?"

"There was a Civilian Public Service camp right close by here, in Warner, New Hampshire," said Gigi.

As Randy turned into the driveway, he said, "I didn't know that."

"There's a lot you don't know, Randy, dear," Gigi said, patting him lightly on the arm. "The men in those camps often worked nine-hour days, six days a week, and they weren't even paid. As a matter of fact, *they* had to pay the government thirty-five dollars a month for their room and board."

"What sort of work did they do?" Randy asked.

"I don't know about all of them, but I do know that in some cases, the men weren't doing much else but busy work—clearing brush, that sort of thing. Not work of national importance at all. So sometimes a man would be driven to try to find other ways to prove to himself and to the world that he wasn't a coward. He'd go and volunteer for tasks that no one else wanted to do."

"If I didn't go to war, that's what I would do," said Randy.

"Do you really think so?" Gigi sounded exasperated. "Do you really think you'd sign up to be an attendant in a mental hospital or volunteer to be a medical guinea pig?"

"What do you mean?" We were at the house now. Randy stopped the car and put on the parking brake and then turned and gave Gigi his complete attention.

I pressed myself as close to the front seat as I could get.

"In the last big war, some of the conscientious objectors contracted diseases like malaria or hepatitis and pneumonia on purpose," said Gigi, "in order to help doctors find a cure for them. They allowed themselves to be covered with lice or be sprayed with DDT. Some even starved themselves in experiments to see what malnutrition would do to them—and for all that, those men were still called names, like yellow-bellies—"

"That's what they call people now who don't want to fight," Randy burst in angrily.

"And some young men," Gigi went on as if Randy hadn't spoken, "decided they could be useful by going to work in the Japanese camps! Imagine that!" she exclaimed. "After the Japanese bombed Pearl Harbor, when Japan was clearly our *enemy*, imagine how most Americans felt about someone who was working to *help* them. Bombing Pearl Harbor was truly an act of evil."

"What is a Japanese camp, Gigi?" I heard my own voice come out in a little squeak.

Gigi turned around to look at me. "Oh my Lord, Holly. I forgot you were here. I shouldn't be talking like this." But she turned quickly back to Randy and started up again. "My point in telling you all this, Randy, is that you need to be more careful as you go out into the world and speak your mind. People have very, very strong feelings on the subject, and I don't want you—Randy, you have to understand—your uncle Jesse—" I held my breath. But she sort of gulped and seemed unable to go on.

Randy sat very still, staring straight ahead, both hands gripping the wheel. His knuckles had turned knobby and white. "Mrs. McCloskey said I look like Uncle Jesse."

"Mrs. McCloskey! She's just an old troublemaker, always has been." But then Gigi added softly, "You do look like him, and he was a very handsome boy."

"She also said he had some funny notions. Gigi—there's something I don't understand at all. Uncle Jesse—was he—when did he join up? And was he in the army, navy, or what?"

Gigi seem to shrink into herself. "I've got a roast in the oven, Randy, dear, that I must see to—perhaps we can talk more about this another time."

"I'm sorry I upset you, Gigi, I didn't mean to." Randy brushed a hand across his eyes. "I just can't help it—I seem to upset everyone these days."

Gigi patted Randy's arm again. "It does occur to me that you might have this war and your mother and father all mixed up together." She sounded more like herself again, warm and comforting. "You'll sort it out, Randy, I know you will. Just please remember in the meantime that your grandfather fought in the first war, and it ruined his health permanently, and your father and your uncles fought in the second one."

"All of them, Gigi?"

Then Gigi said, very quietly, "That's enough for now, Randy."

She opened the car door and climbed out. Randy groaned, his head still resting against the steering wheel. I squeezed into the front and sat next to him.

"What is a Japanese camp?" I asked again.

Randy slowly raised his head. "After the Japanese bombed Pearl Harbor, our government rounded up people of Japanese descent who were living on the West Coast and put them into camps," he said. His voice sounded strained and tired. "Many of them were actually American citizens."

"Camps? Like concentration camps?" I was shocked. We'd learned about the Nazi concentration camps at school, and I'd read *The Diary of Anne Frank*. "We had *those* in the United States?"

"Not exactly—they didn't kill people the way they did in the German camps, but the Japanese were stripped of all their rights, and they were made to pick up and leave their homes with very little notice and with not many possessions. A lot of people were working on farms or in restaurants and stores, and they had to leave their businesses and go and live in the middle of nowhere."

"But *why*?"

Randy tugged on his beard. "Fear. The bombing of Pearl Harbor traumatized people. They thought all the Japanese living in the area were spies. But the truth is, Holly, even before Pearl Harbor, a lot of people didn't like the Japanese being in the United States. There was a law that the first generation of Japanese people who came over from Japan couldn't even own land or become citizens."

"But *why*?" I said again. The unfairness of it didn't make sense to me.

Randy shook his head. "They were very successful at whatever they turned a hand to. Hardworking and resourceful. Made them a threat to the people who were already there. But truthfully, I think their worst crime was the color of their skin." He opened his door and started climbing out of the car.

I watched Randy make his way toward the house. He walked slowly, slightly bent over, as if he were carrying all the troubles of the world on his shoulders. I felt a stab of sadness. Randy used to run everywhere he went. Maybe Ivy was right. Maybe it would be better if we never had to grow up.

Holly

7

As Grandpa liked to say, it was raining horses and elephants. Gigi stuck her head into the Tower Room and said, "Since you won't be able to do much outside today, Holly and Ivy, why don't you come with me this morning to Mrs. LaMare's?"

Gigi was good friends with Mrs. LaMare, the old lady who used to be the postmistress of Otterville. She was ninety-something and still lived alone in a house down the road from Otter Lake House, and when she could, Gigi bought groceries for her.

After breakfast, Ivy and I climbed into Gigi's woodie. We had to drive about twenty miles to get to the grocery store in Munson, which was more of a town than Otterville, and then back to Mrs. LaMare's ramshackle old farmhouse. Ivy and I, carrying two bags each and hurrying through the rain, followed Gigi up the porch stairs to the front door.

Gigi opened the door and yelled in. "Hello, Clare, we're here."

A skinny gray cat came to the door, and then Mrs. LaMare. Her face looked like the bark of an old tree, full of ridges and cracks. Her washed-out blue eyes gazed blankly out at us.

"Hello, Clare," Gigi said loudly. "We're here to bring your groceries. You remember my two granddaughters Holly and Ivy."

Mrs. LaMare's face broke into a thousand creases. "Come in, come in," she said in a creaky voice. "Why, look, it's young Jenny."

I looked at Gigi, confused.

"No, no," said Gigi cheerfully. "This is Jenny's daughter, Holly. She's my granddaughter. And this is Ivy—she's also my granddaughter. You remember them, Clare. They've just gotten bigger and older, so you might not recognize them."

"Holly and Ivy, aren't those clever names?" asked Mrs. LaMare. "Twins, are you? I recollect twins run in your family, Gigi. Now, how old would those darling boys be now?" Ivy and I looked at each other. Mrs. LaMare had really gone downhill since the last time we'd seen her.

"I'll just put your groceries away," Gigi said briskly. "You girls can entertain Mrs. LaMare while I do that."

"Let me show you girls my stamp collection," said Mrs. LaMare.

Mrs. LaMare's stamp collection was famous in the Greenwood family. Mom had loved poring over it when she was a little girl. She even told me once she thought her interest in art history began in Mrs. LaMare's living room, as she was looking at the little pictures of animals from foreign lands or the kings and queens of other countries. Mom said a stamp album was a portable art gallery.

We browsed through the pages of the big stamp album, and then, like always, Mrs. LaMare had us look in the back at her collection of covers, which were stamps that were still glued to their envelopes. "Stamps," Mrs. LaMare said, as she always did, "are more valuable when they are still on their envelopes with the postmarks." But this time she added, "Those twins liked looking at my stamp collection just as much as you do."

Ivy and I glanced at each other.

"Are you talking about Jake and Jesse?" I asked.

"Jake and Jesse," Mrs. LaMare repeated. "Yes, those were their names. Jake was the practical one. Jesse had his head in the clouds. A worry to his parents, that one. Went off to California to go to school instead of to his father's college."

"California?" I asked.

"Oh, yes, he was all wrapped up in that Japanese friend of his, that student over to the college. Can't recollect his name. The one your father was so upset about."

"Do you mean my *father* or my *grandfather*?" I asked. And then I knew. "Was the Japanese friend's name Kiyoshi?"

"What are you talking about?" Ivy asked.

But Gigi came in just at that moment and told us it was time to go.

"Who were you talking about in there?" asked Ivy as we were driving away. "Ki—something."

"No one," I said. I was in the front seat next to Gigi. I turned around and made a face at Ivy. She looked confused, but she didn't ask any more questions.

"You're always very sweet to sit and visit with Mrs. LaMare," said Gigi.

"What a wonderful woman she was in her prime—and a very good friend to me during the war years. Also very discreet as the postmistress of this town. So many letters passing through her hands and never a gossip, like some I knew. But I'm worried about her now. She's slipping more and more into the past. I wish she would go and live with her daughter, but she's so proud of living on her own."

I sat there, staring at Gigi's profile. I was pretty sure she was sixty-eight. Her hands on the steering wheel were veiny and wrinkly, but at least they weren't claws like Mrs. LaMare's. I felt a clutching in my stomach. I didn't want Gigi ever getting as old as Mrs. LaMare.

I turned over what Mrs. LaMare had told us, wondering what would be safest to ask. She had talked quite a bit to Randy the other morning. Maybe she would talk to me.

"Gigi, would you mind if I asked you a question?"

Gigi turned slightly to look at me. "I don't think I'd mind, but I won't know unless you ask."

I gripped the bottom edges of my shorts, holding on to them for strength. "Did Uncle Jesse go to school in California?"

"Holly!" Ivy leaned forward from the backseat and punched me on the back of my shoulder.

Gigi cleared her throat. "Did Mrs. LaMare tell you that?" she asked.

"Yes," I said.

"Well, yes, he did."

I gripped my shorts even harder. "Okay, here's another question." I knew even as the words were forming in my mouth that I shouldn't speak them. But the pressure was too great. I had to know. "Gigi, please tell us. How did Uncle Jesse die?"

"Holly!" Ivy said again, and Gigi didn't answer. She kept her eyes on the road, staring straight in front of her. The windshield wipers went *clack, clack, clack.* I pictured the *Ginny G* turning in circles, a black head bobbing in the water. Finally, Gigi said, "There are reasons why it's better for me not to talk about Uncle Jesse's death. I'm sorry, Holly."

My eyes filled up. Gigi reached over and patted me as tears spilled out of my eyes. She said, "It's okay, Holly. You caught me off-guard, that's all. Some difficult things happened a long time ago, but there's really not much good that will come of speaking about them."

I covered my face with an arm, and the windshield wipers went *clack clack clack*.

"I have to stop at the post office and then at Hutchings' to get a few things I forgot to get in town," Gigi said as if nothing had just happened. "You and Ivy may come in and pick out some penny candy."

But as Gigi and I opened the doors of the station wagon, Ivy sat with her arms crossed, pressing herself into the backseat.

"Are you coming, Ivy?" Gigi asked.

In a tight little voice, Ivy said, "No."

I followed Gigi into the post office. There was a photograph hanging on the wall of Mrs. LaMare when she'd been a lot younger. Her eyes were bright blue, and she looked pretty and vivacious.

Gigi finished getting the mail, and then we went into Hutchings'. The door gave its familiar jingle as we opened it. Mr. Hutchings nodded his white head at us and said, "Mawnin' to ya," in his New Hampshire twang. I stood in front of the glass case of penny candy and picked out red licorice for me and root beer barrels for Ivy.

Waiting for Gigi, I wandered to the back of the store. Up on the wall, above the upright wood-burning stove, there was a chart showing the dates when the lake had frozen up and broken up. As I stood studying it, the door jingled open again, and I heard a voice greeting Mr. Hutchings. Then a tall guy about Randy's age appeared at the back of the store where I was standing. "You're one of the Greenwood grandchildren, aren't you?" he asked.

"I'm Holly," I said.

"Of course! Hi, Holly! Remember me? Will Brown." I recognized him then. The Browns owned the marina at our end of the lake. Will was a little older than Randy, but they had been friends, and Ivy and I were still friendly with Will's younger brother, Ned. After high school, Will had moved to Maine, and we hadn't seen him for a few years.

Will looked like someone who worked outside. His face was ruddy, and his hair was almost the same color as pine needles. Not green ones, of course, but orangey-brown like the ones that have fallen to the ground. His eyes were very blue. He was so good-looking, and I could feel myself blush.

"Ready, Holly?" Gigi called from the door. Then she saw Will. "Oh,

Will! It's been so long!" He shook her hand, and then the two of them got to talking about how he'd been working in a boatyard up in Maine, but he was home now for a while, figuring out the next step.

"College, maybe," he said, "if I can swing it. And say, I built myself my own sailboat while I was up there. Brought it back with me. I'll take the kids out sailing if you'd like."

"That would be wonderful, Will," said Gigi. "Jake is always trying to get everyone sailing. Without much success, I'm afraid."

Back in the car, I said to Ivy, "We met Will Brown in there. He's back from Maine."

Ivy didn't say anything. She just nodded slightly. I knew she was mad at me for bringing up Uncle Jesse to Gigi. But the whole ride back to Otter Lake House, I thought much more about Will Brown's blue eyes than about anything else.

"Let's go up to the loft and play something," I said to Ivy as Gigi pulled into the driveway.

We climbed out of the car, and then there was a moment when Ivy and I stood in the pouring rain facing each other. She crammed her hands into her pockets and hunched her shoulders. Her face was drawn tight and her eyes were narrow slits. "You just really upset Gigi," she said. "You shouldn't have asked about Uncle Jesse." She turned and ran off.

I stood in the driveway and stared straight up at the tops of the pines. The rain felt good against my burning face. Ivy had been mad at me other times, but I'd never, ever seen her this mad. I wasn't sure what to do or where to go. I wandered into the barn, where Grandpa and the uncles and boys were working on the *Ginny G*. Uncle John and my cousin Peter were there. The British Faction must have arrived while we were at Mrs. LaMare's.

Uncle John was my favorite uncle. He was tall and good-looking in a Gregory Peck sort of way, and you could tell he liked kids. He liked helping us put on the Greenwood family play at the end of every August. He laughed a lot and told good stories. He had directed plays in New York and London and now he had his own theater company in Boston, but you'd never know he was sort of famous. He never bragged or acted better than anyone. He came over now and gave me a big hug, and that made me feel better.

I was glad to see Peter, too. He was wearing glasses now, and he looked owlier than last summer. He had spent his last year of high school living in England with his English grandparents. He had also grown a lot since the summer before. Everyone seemed to be shooting up in this family except for me.

Peter came over and gave me a hug, too, but almost right away both Uncle John and Peter returned to the motorboat. Grandpa, Uncle John, Uncle Jimmy, and the boys were all standing like surgeons, peering into the open hatch of the motorboat, making comments, tinkering with the engine.

I felt both invisible and in the way.

Piano music came pouring out of the house. Ivy could play the piano when she was mad or upset, but I didn't know what to do with myself.

Aunt Felicity was in the living room. She said hello in her scrumptious English accent, and she gave me a big hug, and then Tucker came in, having had enough of the motorboat. He and the twins and I set up a game of Monopoly on the table. Tally used the top hat as her token, which didn't seem right because the top hat was usually Ivy's token. Tigs needed help figuring out the money, and I didn't feel like helping her. I ended up giving the twins the candy I had bought at Hutchings' to make up for my impatience with them.

Sam wandered in. He watched us play for a minute, and then he said, "Did you know the British Secret Service had a special edition of Monopoly made for prisoners who were held by the Nazis? They hid compasses and maps and money in them to help them escape."

"Count on you to know something like that, Sam," said Tucker.

Uncle Jake came in and made a fire in the big stone fireplace. I realized he was the only uncle (besides Dad, of course) who wasn't helping with the motorboat. My stomach lurched. It had to be because of what had happened to Uncle Jesse.

I could hear Aunt Sandy's muffled voice going on and on. She was stuffed into the little telephone closet again. She was always talking to her friends in New Jersey.

We quit the game, and Tucker started reading an old science fiction magazine. The twins played circus with stuffed animals under the table. Aunt Kate was getting close to finishing a sweater she was knitting for Tina, and Aunt Felicity sat on the couch reading a mystery. Gigi came in with the mail. "Postcard for you, Holly. Trolley cars in San Francisco."

Seeing Mom's familiar handwriting, I grabbed the card from Gigi, ran up the stairs to the Tower Room, and sat in the middle of the floor and read it.

> It's fun teaching a course with Dad. It makes me think we should do this more often. This is a fascinating city, but my research is not going so well, and we miss the pine trees and the birches, and more than anything, we miss you and everyone else at Otter Lake. Can't wait to be there. I know you must be having a wonderful time with Ivy and all the cousins.
>
> > Hugs, hugs and kisses,
> > Mom and Dad

I looked around at the dirty socks and wet towels and the clothes spilling out of my half-unpacked suitcase. I finished unpacking and then started picking up books, toenail polish (Tina's), suntan lotion (Tina's), and shampoo. (Tina's also, although she had washed her hair with a raw egg in the morning. It had made her long light-brown hair really shiny.)

I scooped up a scattered deck of cards and counted them, making sure they were all there. I put my dirty clothes in the hamper. Ivy, of course, always hung up her clothes or folded them and put them away in her bureau. She put her socks and underwear in the top drawer and sweaters in the bottom one.

I climbed up on my bunk bed with the postcard. For a moment I was really mad at myself for not going to California with Mom and Dad. California! Where I'd just found out Jesse had gone to college.

It wouldn't have hurt me to miss a few weeks at Otter Lake. Then I was mad at Mom for not being here. Why did she have to teach this summer? And Dad, too. Why did he have to be teaching so far away? He'd promised to show me how to identify edible mushrooms this summer, and there would hardly be any summer left by the time he got here.

I climbed back down and hunted through my things for some stationery. I sat on the floor and started to write.

Dear Mom and Dad,

Everything's fine here at Otter Lake. Grandpa let Ivy and me fix up an old rowboat that belonged to Uncle Jake and Uncle Jesse. We painted it in rainbow stripes like it used to be. Maybe you remember it? Ivy and I rowed out to the islands.

Peter is here. He has a funny English accent now just like Miranda had when she came back from her year in England. We haven't seen Miranda even once yet. She's living at the Glover Summer Theater with all the other college-aged interns. I hope she's going to come soon and tell us what the end-of-summer Greenwood play is going to be.

I stopped for a moment and sat there trying to remember what Mom had told me about Uncle Jesse. Not much. He was nice. He died in World War II. He had a short but good life. And that was pretty much it. I started writing again.

Mom, will you please tell me what you know about Uncle Jesse dying? Did something terrible happen when Uncle Jake and Jesse were out in the *Ginny G*? Please, please tell me what you know about him.

Also, did you know a Japanese boy named Kiyoshi? What sorrow did he bring to our family? Was he friends with Uncle Jesse?

I tore up the letter and started again. I didn't want to upset Mom when she was so far away. I wrote everything the same until the part about Uncle Jesse. I wrote,

Please can you tell me some things about Uncle Jesse? I think because of going out in the old rowboat, I feel this strong connection to him. I know that sounds strange, but it's true. I'd really like to know more about him. If it's not upsetting to tell me. Also, I am wondering what you're researching out there? I wish I'd asked you more about it before you left. Dad, don't forget you're going to show me how not to eat a poisonous mushroom.

Love,
Holly

I figured I could ask Mom about Kiyoshi when I saw her.

I climbed back up on my bed and stared at the rabbit-deer knot again. I remembered playing circus with Ivy under the table, just like Tigs and Tally were doing now. For one whole summer we played Peter Pan, and the one after that was the Robin Hood summer, and the one after that we were the Sons of Liberty, and we took all the tea bags out of the pantry and threw them into the lake. I missed being able to pretend things with Ivy. We were too old, or too *something*. I didn't really know what it was that made it impossible to pretend anymore.

I could hear someone flushing the toilet in the bathroom below the Tower Room.

I knew what all the sounds in the house were.

Squeaks: water faucets. Scrapes: wooden doors. Creaks: front stairs. Thumps: back stairs.

I couldn't stand being in the house one more minute. I put the letter in an envelope and took it downstairs for Gigi, who knew Mom and Dad's address in San Francisco.

Ivy's diary

I was mad at Holly all day today. She can be so dumb sometimes, asking Gigi about Jesse. I could see how Gigi froze up when Holly asked her about him. It was like she stabbed Gigi in the heart with a dagger. I wish Holly would learn to keep her mouth shut.

At supper she sat across the table from me as usual, and I could tell she wanted me not to be mad at her anymore. To tell the truth, I wasn't really even thinking about her anymore. I was just feeling really lousy about my piano playing. I'm not progressing—just playing the same old way over and over again. So I still wasn't in a very good mood.

Grandpa served the food, and then Gigi lifted her fork so we could begin eating. And then pretty soon everyone was gabbing away and talking like always.

Peter is here now. He sat at the table in between the twins, and they kept asking him to say things with an English accent. Every time he did, he set them off laughing.

"Say *mashed potatoes* with an English accent," Tigs begged Peter.

"My English gran always says *smashed* potatoes," said Peter.

Tally said very loudly, and in a very bad fake English accent, "Please pass the smashed potatoes."

Holly started to giggle. And so did I. I couldn't help it. Tigs said, "These *smashed* potatoes are simply smashing," and that set Holly and me off again, and now the twins were laughing so hard, Uncle Jimmy said, "Tigs and Tally, you may be excused from the table."

"From the house," said Aunt Kate. "Go outside."

"Holly and Ivy, too," said Uncle Jake.

Holly muttered, "Smashed potatoes," under her breath as we ran out of the house, and that set me off again.

We started to run and didn't stop until we came to the Sunbird.

Holly and I said at the same exact time, "*Grant us our wish, O Sunbird Tree, and we will be grateful for eternity.*"

My wish: *Please don't let me get so mad at Holly again.*

"Uma cotcha walla," she said, reaching for my hand.

I answered, "Uma cotcha walla," and we did the Walla Walla handshake.

It wasn't raining anymore. Smoke from the fire up at the house drifted down. It smelled cozy. The air was misty and made the pine tree look like an Oriental painting. The ferns were wet, sopping my sneakers and the bottoms of my jeans, but I didn't care because Holly and I were friends again.

But when we came up to the house, Miranda was standing outside with a cape draped around her shoulders.

We yelled, "Miranda!" We were so happy to see her, we ran up to hug her, but she put out a hand to stop us.

"I am the king," she said. "The grass is green. The sky is blue. The birds do fly, and the fish do swim. My people do walk upon the earth, and here come two of my subjects now." Miranda pointed at us. "Kneel, peasants, in the presence of thy mighty king."

Holly said, "But, my liege, we are your long-lost cousins, wandering in the forest all these long years. We have only just now trod the right path to find thee."

"What proof have you of this bold and reckless claim?" asked Miranda.

I said, "By my troth, O king, thou shalt know us by the mole on our right knee."

"You *both* have moles on your right knee?" Miranda asked. "Zounds! Come forward, cousins!" Miranda flung off the cape, which was actually one of Gigi's tablecloths.

Holly asked her what she was doing, and Miranda said she was working on the end-of-summer play, *The Prince and the Pauper*. "Dad said it was the first Greenwood play they put on when they were kids. It was the start of the glorious family tradition."

Holly said, "I *love* that story!" And she started dancing excitedly around Miranda.

My heart sank. A play about twins. I could see what was coming. And sure enough, Miranda said, "As a matter of fact, you two will play the main parts."

I knew it.

Holly was *leaping* around Miranda now, saying, "Really? That's so neat!"

Miranda said, "You'll play the prince, Ivy—you have that noble and royal bearing—and Holly should play the pauper—rough and ready, you know...."

All I could think of was people sitting there looking at me. I don't *want* people looking at me. I said, "Holly and I don't even look alike."

Miranda laughed and said, "You don't have to. Anyhow, you guys are like twins inside."

I said, "Tigs and Tally should play the twins. They're real twins."

"They're only six years old," said Miranda.

I said, "I don't want a big part in the play this summer."

Both Holly and Miranda said, "Ivy!" And Miranda said, "It's just for fun—for the family. You can even hold the script if you don't want to learn the lines."

I didn't know how to describe the panic I was feeling. I don't even know why—I've always loved being in the play before. I said, "I have to practice for a piano competition. I can't be in a play."

And now, guess what? Holly is mad at me.

Holly
8

The whole family plus Will and Ned Brown was spread out along the trail on the annual Mount Wigan Expedition. Randy, Peter, Sam, and Will were way out in front, and then came the uncles, who had all managed a day off, and then Grandpa. Grandpa was still such a strong hiker—you'd never know he was seventy-something. Ivy, Ned, Tucker, and I were next. The aunts and Gigi and the twins walked behind us, and trailing way behind, talking a mile a minute, were Tina and Miranda.

I heard Aunt Felicity say, "Where is Sandy?" and Aunt Kate said, "She said she was going to Concord today." Aunt Felicity sniffed and said, "Is she *shopping*? Who goes *shopping* when they could be hiking Mount Wigan?"

I glanced at Ivy. She must have heard them. She pulled right into her shell, and I was glad Ned was along for the hike.

"Say, did you know your folks are hiring Will to give you guys sailing lessons?" Ned asked me in his New Hampshire twang. "I sure would like to take 'em, too, but Dad's got me working for him from sunup to sundown." Grinning, he pushed back his hair with one hand.

His hair wasn't long or short, just regular, and a little messy. Ned never paid attention to fashion. He was wearing what he always wore—a white T-shirt and old shorts with paint stains on them. His sneakers were paint-splattered, too, with holes in them.

Then I realized Ned's arms and legs were muscley. And *hairy*. When had Ned gotten so muscley and hairy? Right there on the trail, I felt *shy*. With Ned. For Pete's sake, this was Ned. I had known Ned before we could walk. We'd learned to swim together at our beach.

"I don't know about sailing lessons," I said. "Mostly, I don't like lessons—I'd rather figure things out for myself."

"Yeah," Ned agreed. He grinned again, and I could tell he was feeling shy with me, too.

When we got to the top, the white-throated sparrows sang to us, the mica sparkled in the granite, and the scrubby little balsam trees smelled like Christmas trees. I was so proud that my own two legs had carried me to the top. It was very clear, and we could see a lot of other mountains, even Mount Washington. In the other direction, we could just make out the Prudential Building in Boston. Carved into the green of the valley was a miniature Otter Lake.

We had PB&J sandwiches and oranges and chocolate bars and watery fruit juice, which we called bug juice. And then we stayed up at the top for a long time. Some of the aunts and uncles and Grandpa took a nap while the kids played hide-and-seek around the boulders. When it was time to go back down, Ned and Tucker and I ran all the way, leaping from rock to rock like goats. Ivy followed more slowly. She kept moving her fingers and talking to herself. I think she was practicing the piano as she walked along.

At the picnic and parking area halfway up the mountain, Uncle Jake and Uncle John made a fire in a big stone fireplace. The aunts unpacked picnic baskets and spread tablecloths on the tables. We played a fun soccer game with a ball Will had brought along. Uncle Jimmy was the only grown-up who played with us, but he spent the whole time giving Tucker pointers on how to kick the ball and who to pass it to and I think Tucker wished he'd just go away and leave him alone.

Then we ate hot dogs, hamburgers, potato chips, Aunt Felicity's potato salad, Aunt Kate's coleslaw, and Gigi's pickles.

Uncle John said to me, "Shame Jenny and her pie-making skills aren't here for this. And too bad Mike isn't here. He loves the Mount Wigan Expedition. What are your parents doing in California, anyway?"

"They're teaching an art history course together," I said. "And Mom says they're researching something they can only find out in California."

"Must be important to keep them away from Otter Lake," Uncle John said.

"They'll be back before everyone leaves," I said. I knew he would like to hear that. He and Aunt Felicity and Mom and Dad got along very well.

Then he spent a long time asking me questions about my school production of A *Midsummer Night's Dream*, and how did I play the role of Puck, and what did I think about kids doing Shakespeare. He listened really carefully and nodded a lot and made me feel as if I had interesting things to say.

And it was all I could do not to blurt out, "Uncle John, what happened to Uncle Jesse in the *Ginny G*?"

But I didn't want to ruin the Mount Wigan Expedition.

At the end of the meal, Grandpa brought out the old ice cream maker. We took turns cranking it, making real strawberry ice cream, and then we sat licking away, watching the sunset. There were streaks of red everywhere, and then more red, so it looked as if the sky were on fire.

"Look at that sun," said Will. "It looks like the Japanese flag."

"Good way to ruin a perfectly good sunset," said Uncle Jake.

Will turned to him, surprised. "Sorry," he said.

The blue started to deepen, and then it turned black, and the first star came out, only it wasn't a star, but Venus, the planet. And then a real star popped out, and then another and another. I tried to see if I could catch the stars appearing, but I couldn't. All at once they were just *there*.

And then as we roasted marshmallows, Randy brought out a guitar and we sang songs by Peter, Paul, and Mary—"If I Had a Hammer" and "Lemon Tree" and "Where Have All the Flowers Gone?" We sang Bob Dylan's "Blowin' in the Wind." Then Randy said he'd sing us some of the gospel songs he'd learned when he was in Mississippi last summer.

"*Oh, freedom, before I'll be a slave,*" Randy sang, "*I'll be buried in my grave, and go home to my Lord and be free.*" His voice was so strong and emotional, it made me shiver. He sang another one where the chorus was "*We shall not be moved.*" And we were clapping and singing really loudly by the end. Then we all sang "We Shall Overcome" and I started to cry when we came to "*Deep in my heart, I do believe, that we shall overcome someday.*" It made me want to overcome all the bad the things that have ever happened in the world, like the Japanese camps.

We finished up with good oldies like "I've Been Working on the Railroad." And, of course, the twins' favorite, "I Know an Old Lady Who Swallowed a Fly."

Ned and Tucker and I liked our marshmallows burned black so the insides turned gooey, and Ivy toasted hers slowly, slowly, slowly, so they turned a perfect golden brown.

I noticed that Tina was sitting right beside Will the entire time we were around the campfire.

When we got home it was really late. I went upstairs and brushed my teeth, but even so, the charcoal taste of the marshmallows stayed in my mouth. I liked that. It made me feel as if the perfect day wasn't quite over. I climbed up onto the top bunk, feeling peaceful. Tina and Ivy hadn't come up yet. Since I was an only child, I liked being by myself sometimes.

And then Ivy did come in. She ducked right into her bunk, but not before I saw that she'd been crying.

"Ivy? You okay?" I hung my head over the edge of the bed.

She was lying facedown with her head in her pillow, and she didn't answer.

Then there was all this clomping up the stairs to the Tower Room, and Tina came barging in singing at the top of her lungs.

"I *love him, I love him, I love him, and where he goes, I'll follow, I'll follow, I'll follow*—I *will follow* HIM."

I pointed to Ivy's bed and put a finger to my lips. Tina broke off singing and said, "Oops, sorry, hope I didn't wake anyone." Then she said, "Well, nighty-night, everyone," and, still humming loudly, stood in front of the bureau mirror, brushing and brushing her hair with a huge smile on her face.

Ivy's diary

I'm sitting in the bathroom writing by flashlight.

Mom and Dad called Sam and me into their bedroom when we got back from the mountain tonight. Mom said we have to go to boarding school. Sam and me, that is.

I knew it! I knew that was what she and Dad had been doing—sneaking around behind our backs and going off to look at schools. I ought to tell Aunt Felicity that Mom wasn't shopping for clothes, she was shopping for *schools*.

Sam asked, "Why? Why do we have to go to boarding school?" Mom said, "Your father and I don't think the schools are good enough at home." Dad didn't say anything. He was staring at his shoes, looking uncomfortable.

Sam said, "You just don't want me at home because you can't control me," and Mom said, "Don't be silly."

Anyway, we have to go and look at schools while we're up here.

I don't know what I think. Do I have a choice, anyway?

Sam said in the hall after we left their bedroom, "It's because they're going to get a divorce, I bet you anything." So he's been thinking that, too.

He looked as white as a sheet and there were tears in his eyes. I don't think I've seen Sam cry since the time he almost cut his finger off.

Divorce. All these chords started crashing around in my head. While we were hiking Wigan today, I went over the Mozart piece in my mind. I thought I'd figured out the hard part in the middle section, and I even thought, *I've almost got the piece now and competing won't be so bad.* But now I feel as if all those notes don't really fit together anymore. Nothing makes sense.

Holly
9

I woke up in the middle of the night having to go to the bathroom. It was really dark out—usually there was some light coming in through all the windows, but tonight I couldn't even see my own hands.

I groped around, found the edge of the bunk, and lowered myself down, feeling for the floor with my toes. Holding my arms out, I started walking and banged right into a wall. I scrabbled around and felt the latch on the door. The door seemed harder than usual to open. The bottom edge of it scraped against the floor. I reached in, sliding my hand along the wall for the switch. I couldn't understand why it wasn't there, but I stepped in anyway, inching along, and banged my shins on something and fell face-forward.

Yikes.

It took me a second to sit up. It was still so dark. I couldn't tell what was around me, walls or ceiling or anything. I reached out to pat the thing I had tripped over. It felt like a trunk. It slowly dawned on me that I'd gotten turned around. I was in the storage closet, in with the old bed frames and boxes and trunks. So now all I had to do was get out of there.

But the dark was too dark. It was like a black lake pressing me down. If I moved a muscle, I would bump into Uncle Jesse, because I could sense him with me in the black lake, too. I put my head down on my knees and squeezed my eyes shut tight. If I could shut out the dark, I could shut out Uncle Jesse.

I heard a noise behind me. My eyes flew open, and still all I could see was the black lake, and Uncle Jesse trying to swim underwater, and the propellers of the motorboat churning the water, and—I started screaming.

A beam of light swept toward me. "Holly! Is that you? Holly! What are you doing in there?"

And there was Tina in her nightgown, holding out her flashlight like Nancy Drew.

"I got up to go to the bathroom," I said, "and I couldn't see anything, and I got all turned around."

Tina started to giggle.

"And I—I thought—I thought I saw a ghost."

I expected Tina to laugh some more, but all she said was, "Geez, Hol, you are so freaky. Stop talking like that. The electricity isn't working, and it's wicked dark. That's freaky enough." She came in and sat on the box I had tripped on. I felt a hundred times better. Tina was so *normal*. She swung the beam of the flashlight around. I could see a few spiky nails sticking down from the beams above my head. Good thing I was short.

"Don't tell anyone I said that," I said. "About the ghost."

"Not even Ivy?" Tina asked.

"No," I said, almost too quickly. I could just imagine Ivy's reaction if I brought up Uncle Jesse again.

"How come? I thought you and Ivy were as tight as Tom and Jerry. Rocky and Bullwinkle. John Lennon and Paul McCartney."

I suddenly wondered if Tina sometimes felt left out by Ivy and me.

"You could do more stuff with us, Tina, like going out rowing and things. It's fun."

"Nothing against you, Hol, or anything, but number one, I'd be bored out my skull rowing with you guys, and number two, Ivy's just not my type. She's so into classical music, you know?"

"You don't like her because she's into classical music?"

"No, it's not really that. I don't mean to bad-mouth her, but honestly, a lot of times she acts like she's better than other people. And Uncle Jake and Aunt Sandy—"

"Shhh, keep your voice down, she'll hear you."

"They're such a drag," said Tina, whispering now. "It's gross how they're wigging out all the time right in front of us. Mom says they might—you know—the *d* word."

"*What*?"

"Gosh, Holly, didn't that ever cross your mind? They fight all the time."

"I know they fight, but—"

"I knew it was going to be awful this summer without Miranda here," Tina broke in. "I *begged* Mom and Dad to let me stay home and lifeguard at the pool, but they said no, it means so much to Gigi and Grandpa for us to come up here. They're saying they might let me go home early, though, or maybe some of my friends can come up."

Each thing Tina said gave me a little shock. She'd rather *lifeguard* at a *swimming pool* than be at the lake? She was thinking of going home *early*? Or her friends might come up to Otter Lake? I'd met some of her friends when we were at her house for Thanksgiving. They were all just as shiny and cool as Tina. I tried to imagine them on the dock or sitting with us at the table. I'd hate that. They'd make me feel like a stranger in my own land.

"You know what, Hol? I can fix your hair tomorrow. Trim the ends, and no offense or anything, but it looks like someone chewed off your bangs."

I ran my fingers through my hair. "I cut my own bangs—they were driving me crazy."

"Oh, Holly, Holly," Tina sighed. "What is the matter with you, child? I can even them up, and then you can put your hair back in barrettes, and it'll make your face look thinner."

"Oh, thanks," I said. "Now you're saying I have a fat face."

"That's not what I meant," said Tina, giggling. "Hey, what is this I'm sitting on, anyway?"

"Some kind of trunk."

"A trunk! Let's see what's inside it."

She slipped off the trunk and held the flashlight while I flipped up the clasps and lifted the lid.

"Whew, mothballs, what a stink!" said Tina.

Holding the flashlight with one hand, she pulled out old sweaters and flannel pants. At the bottom, under the clothes, were a carved wooden box and a pile of old yellow-and-brown photographs. I tried to open the box but couldn't get the lid off.

"There's the dock and the boathouse, and Uncle Jake's sailboat moored out a little ways," said Tina.

"Here's one of Grandpa," I said. "He looks so young!"

"Here's Dad!" Tina squealed. "He used to have so much more hair!"

"Here's one of Mom," I said. I turned the photograph over. In Gigi's handwriting it said, *Otter Lake, 1940.*

"Your mom was so *cute* with all that curly hair. And good gravy, look at Uncle Jake—he was so skinny back then, and here's—O my gosh, that must be Uncle Jesse. You know what? I don't think I've ever seen a picture of him, not ever. I guess he and Jake weren't identical twins. He was a lot cuter than Jake. Look at those dimples. I bet he was a wicked flirt. Oh my God, is that a hickey on his neck?"

"I don't believe you, Tina. It's just a shadow."

"Ha ha, just joshing ya. And here's another one of him. He's all dressed up for church or something—got his best jacket on. It's almost creepy how he looks so much like Randy."

I took the photograph from Tina and stared at it. "He really does," I said. "*Jesse on his Save the Otter Campaign. 1939*," I read out from the back. "Just a few days ago Uncle Jake said something about boys chasing otters in motorboats."

"Here's another of Jesse," said Tina. "He's with this Oriental boy, looking like they're best buddies." She handed me the photograph.

Uncle Jesse was standing on the dock. I guessed he was about Randy's age at the time. He had one arm slung across an Oriental boy's shoulders. Jesse did look like Randy, and the Oriental boy was skinny, with very dark hair. He had a shy smile. On the back, in Gigi's handwriting, it said, *Jesse and Kiyoshi. 1941.*

I stared and stared at the photograph. What sorrow could Kiyoshi possibly have caused? He looked so nice.

"You know what, I'm ready to get out of here," Tina said. "Mothballs are getting to me."

She scrambled out of ahead of me, and I followed, bringing the photographs. I banged against something as I came out, making a lot of noise. "Nice move, Grace," said Tina, and she started laughing hysterically. I couldn't help laughing with her.

"What's going on?" Ivy asked, sitting up.

That made us laugh even more.

"You *guys*."

"Sorry," we both said.

Using Tina's flashlight, I found the bathroom, and then I climbed up into my bed.

"Nighty-night," Tina called out.

"Would you *shut up*?" said Ivy.

"I am *so, so* sorry if we are keeping you from your beauty sleep," said Tina.

I snuggled in under the covers, grateful Tina had found me in the dark.

And we'd found Uncle Jesse. All along he had been there, just as I had imagined.

Ivy's diary

At the table last night everyone was talking about Will Brown giving us sailing lessons, and Sam said in a loud voice that he isn't allowed to take sailing lessons. He has to be tutored in math while everyone else is out having fun so he can pass the entrance tests for boarding school. And that's how it came out that we're going to boarding school. I think Gigi and Grandpa already knew about it, but everyone else seemed shocked.

Aunt Felicity asked about my music, and Mom said the schools we're looking at have fabulous music programs. "But what about the music competition in the fall?" Aunt Felicity wanted to know. "Doesn't Ivy have a teacher she's been studying with?"

Aunt Felicity gave me such a sympathetic look I felt like crying. Mom said she was sure I could find a teacher at my new school. I wanted to ask, *How can you be so sure?*

Aunt Kate said, "I can't imagine sending my children away," and Mom looked daggers at her.

Randy said, "I wish I had been able to go to boarding school, it's a great idea. Sam and Ivy, take it from me—you're the luckiest kids in the world."

Holly was staring up at the ceiling the whole time. I notice she does that every time there's even the slightest hint of an argument. She hates it when people don't get along. She'd last about two seconds if she lived in my family.

Later she said, "Gosh, Ivy, are you really going away to school?"

I said, "If I get in anywhere. They're taking us to look at some schools at the end of the week." She wanted to know how come they want us to go to away to school, and I told her they're saying the schools at home aren't good enough.

I didn't say what I think the real reason is—that Mom and Dad want us to go away so they can get divorced. The thought of it sits like a big stone in my stomach, and I'm afraid to say the word *divorce* out loud, because if I do, it might come true.

This morning after I practiced, I went up to the Tower Room to change into shorts, and Holly was sitting in front of the mirror while Tina played hairdresser. I asked Holly what she was doing, and Holly said she was changing her hairstyle. I said, "I like it the way you always have it."

She said, "But this looks good, don't you think?"

I probably shouldn't have said anything, but I couldn't help it. I said, "I thought we weren't going to change."

She said, "On the inside, not the outside."

I said, "You *are* changing on the inside," and even as the words came out of my mouth, I knew I sounded like a five-year-old.

And Tina, who had ignored me up until then, said, "This is definitely an improvement, and when your bangs grow out, I'll be able to do other stuff. See ya later, alligator, I'm going down to the dock to catch some rays."

She left, and Holly said, "If I want to change my hair, I can, and I don't have to ask your permission."

She left the Tower Room, slamming the door. It made everything rattle.

I DON'T UNDERSTAND HOW EVERYTHING CAN BE SO BAD.

Holly
10

I was sitting on the dock with the sketchbook in my lap trying to paint the shore across the lake. Blue, I notice, is always bluest when it's next to green. Miranda and Peter were sitting near me, talking. The funny thing is, whenever you're doing something like drawing or painting, people don't notice you.

"Let's go camping up on the top of the hill behind the house," Miranda was saying to Peter. "I have so little time off this summer, but I still want to be able to do some Otter Lake things."

"I remember the time you got spooked up there," said Peter. "You thought you saw a ghost, and then you spooked the rest of us, and then we made Randy come back down to the house with us in the middle of the night."

"Randy was so mad at me." Miranda laughed, but then she looked more thoughtful. "I wish he would come camping with us. He's so serious all the time now."

"Randy won't come, but Will Brown is coming," says Peter. "And everyone else, except for the twins, of course."

"Hey, is Ivy okay?" Miranda asked Peter. "I mean, she's so quiet this summer."

"She's always been quiet," said Peter.

"Yeah, but not like this," said Miranda. "I think things between Aunt Sandy and Uncle Jake are getting worse, and she must be going through a hard time."

"Let's not forget to lug water up the hill," said Peter, who, I could tell, didn't want to talk about Aunt Sandy and Uncle Jake. "If we all carry some it won't be so bad."

I closed up the sketchbook, thinking about how I'd yelled at Ivy when Tina was fixing my hair. Of course Ivy was going through a hard time because of her parents. I didn't know why I was being such a jerk to her.

"Golly, Will," said Tina. She batted her eyelashes, and I thought she sounded just like Scarlett O'Hara in *Gone With the Wind*. "What have you got in your knapsack? It looks like you're going on a three-week trek in the wilderness."

"Let's see," said Will, shifting his knapsack. "I got me a railroad car, a couple of cowboys, and the Oregon Trail. And a bottle of fly dope." He took out a little bottle of insect repellant from one of the side pockets and unscrewed the cap. "Perfume from heaven, ma'am," he said, holding it under Tina's nose.

"Get that disgusting stuff away from me," said Tina, squealing.

"I kind of like the smell," said Tucker.

"It reminds me of my boyhood days as a Kentucky lad when me an' Pa used to rub bear grease on us to keep the skeeters from chompin' on our hides."

I loved the way Will made everything fun. He hitched the knapsack onto his back as the rest of us collected our gear, including the water everyone had to carry. And then we set off, striking out for the path behind the house with Peter in the lead. I hung back a little, not wanting to hear Tina flirt with Will. I wished Ned were coming camping with us, but he had to pump gas at the marina. Ivy hung back, too, and as I walked beside her, I tried to think about how to start a good conversation with her.

The path was overgrown, so we had to push away branches and scramble over windfall as we walked.

"Hey, Ives, you want to talk or anything?" I asked.

"No, I don't." The words shot out of Ivy like a bullet. I ducked my head to hide the tears that suddenly welled up in my eyes.

"Sorry," she said after a moment. "I just don't want to talk about stuff right now."

"Okay," I said.

Will was singing at the top of his lungs. "*I love to go a-wandering—*"

"He's always such a loudmouth," said Ivy, scowling.

I walked a bit faster to catch up with the others. It was too hard with Ivy. Every once in a while there was a flicker of our old friendship, but mostly something kept getting in the way.

The path ended in a small clearing near a giant pine. It was the tree Ivy and I could see when we were sitting up in Big Tree. There was a semicircle of rocks, black from having held many fires, and logs were set around it for sitting on. Will collapsed on a log with the knapsack still on his back. He took off his hat and fanned his face.

"You better get more fit if you're going to join up," said Tina.

"You're joining up?" Peter took off his knapsack and stared at Will curiously.

"Thinking about the navy," said Will. "Ticket to college."

"Wow," said Peter. "I was kind of hoping that by *going* to college, I could get out of serving for a while—sorry," he added quickly, "I—"

"No, it's okay. The thing is, I'll like being in the navy."

Peter stood waving bugs out of his eyes, and then he said, "We need firewood. Everyone go and collect two armfuls."

We all went crashing off into the woods. I thought about Will signing up for the navy. I was glad I was a girl and wouldn't ever have to be a soldier. But it was terrible thinking every boy I knew would have to face the draft eventually—Randy and Peter, Sam at some point—Ned. Even Tucker down the line.

I leaned over to pick up another stick and right in front of my eyes, carved into the smooth bark of a beech tree, was another Sunbird. I rubbed my fingers lightly over it, feeling prickles up the back of my neck. I'd have done anything to know who had carved the Sunbirds and what they meant.

Tucker appeared behind me. "I'm on my third armful," he said proudly. "And I started the fire. One match."

"That's great, Tuck."

"Hey, do you think Ivy's okay? I saw her sitting over there." His arms were full, so he tilted his head to show me where. "I don't think she's doing so good."

"I'll go take a look," I said. But after he left, I touched the Sunbird again and made a wish. *Let things between me and Ivy get better.* I looked at her sitting on a log. The sight of her drooping shoulders stopped me cold. Maybe I'd show her the Sunbird later.

The smell of wood smoke and the sound of Will playing his guitar pulled me back to the campfire. It wasn't long before I was busy wrapping potatoes in tinfoil.

Ivy finally joined us in the middle of cooking hot dogs and hamburgers.

"You okay, Ivy?" Miranda asked.

Ivy nodded, and there didn't seem to be anything else to say. We finished up all the food, and sat around the fire, and Miranda told us about *The Comedy of Errors*, the play by Shakespeare she was in. She said she was having trouble with one of her lines, not saying it quite right, so she told us what it was, and everyone tried different ways of saying it. It got really funny, but Ivy still didn't join in.

As it grew dark, the fire burned down to coals. We cut green sticks and roasted marshmallows.

"How about 'Eyes, Eyes, Thousands of Eyes'?" Peter asked. "Randy's not here, so I'll tell it."

"Yes, do, carry on," said Miranda, imitating Peter's English accent.

"Our story takes us into deepest, darkest Africa," Peter began, "where three men journeyed to seek their fortune in a diamond mine."

As we sat in a semicircle on the logs, the fire brought out a glow in everyone's faces. Peter was wearing a red bandana on his head, making him look like a pirate with glasses. With her black curls poking out from her own red bandana, Miranda looked like a Gypsy. Sam sat staring intently into the fire, smiling slightly. Tucker had dirty smudges on his cheeks. Will's hair perfectly matched the pine needles on the ground around us. Tina was sitting next to him and laughing at everything he said. She was wearing a blue bandana folded over neatly like a headband. And Ivy was sitting on a stump slightly outside the circle. I wished she would at least *sit* with everyone.

I drifted in and out of listening, and started thinking about Uncle Jesse—how he and Uncle Jake and Jimmy and John and my mom all had camped up here, too, once upon a time, telling stories.

One by one Peter killed off the three miners, making each death more terrible than the one before, and as he said the final "Eyes, eyes, thousands of eyes," his voice faded into a whisper and everyone clapped.

"You have Randy beat as official ghost-story teller," said Miranda.

Will brought out his guitar again, and we sat around singing. I got up and went over to my sleeping bag. I snuggled into it and looked up at the bits of sky between the crisscross of pine needles. The stars were out now, as big as fists. Miranda and Will sang "Four Strong Winds" in two-part harmony. It was really pretty. Then I tucked my head inside my sleeping bag to get away from the drone of a mosquito. The last things I heard before falling asleep were the muffled voices of Will and Tina. They seem to be getting along like—well, like Tom and Jerry, Rocky and Bullwinkle, John Lennon and Paul McCartney.

And the next thing I knew, I was in a diamond mine looking for Uncle Jesse. I was in a maze, walking and walking, looking for the end of the tunnel. With every step the walls closed in, until there was almost no space to walk at all. I was beginning to suffocate. *Let me out! Let me out!* I screamed in the dream, and I woke myself up. I opened my eyes. I was in the black lake again. Nothing but darkness. I tried to sit up. I couldn't move. Something was pinning my arms against my sides. I was about to start screaming for real. Then I heard a voice, calm and soothing.

"Your head is facing the bottom of the sleeping bag, and you're twisted up in it."

I lay as still as I could, my heart pounding too hard.

"Start backing out, feet first," the voice said.

I kicked and rolled and groped my way out of the sleeping bag. Sitting up, I gulped in a couple of deep breaths of cool air. All around me were lumps of sleeping people. The fire was a glimmer of embers. I straightened out the sleeping bag and lay down on top of it, face up to the sky. The stars hung on the tips of the tree branches like Christmas tree ornaments. I was afraid to get back in the bag, afraid to close my eyes.

"Don't worry," said the voice. "I'll watch over you."

I climbed back into the bag and closed my eyes.

It wasn't until I woke up in the morning that I wondered about the voice. I sat right up. "You didn't talk to me in the middle of the night, did you?" I asked Peter.

"Huh?"

"I was tangled up in my sleeping bag, and someone talked to me."

"Not me," says Peter. "I slept like a baby."

"Will?"

Will raised his eyebrows. "What? Did I talk in my sleep?"

"*Anyone?*" I glanced around at the group. Everyone was looking groggy and grubby.

"Holly heard the ghost," said Miranda, pleased. "I always said there was a ghost up here, but no one ever believed me!"

I clutched my arms around my knees, feeling strange.

Ivy's diary

We went camping up on the hill last night.

Everyone was sitting around the campfire, talking and laughing and stuff, and I kept thinking about how shy I feel with everyone, and I don't know what to say to people. It's like I'm living in a land where I'm alone because no one speaks my language. Maybe I've always lived there, but I didn't realize it before because Holly used to be there with me, and we spoke our special language together. Now I can see she likes being with Tina and Ned and Will and everyone more than with me. She knows how to get along in their land.

But then a little later when I was lying in my sleeping bag, everything was quiet, and this piece of music floated into my mind. At camp this summer, the Japanese teacher, Tōru, played us one of his own compositions. It was a mix of Eastern and Western music, and it had this really pretty Japanese song mixed into it. I liked it so much I went up to Tōru afterward and asked him where I could buy the score, and he said I didn't have to buy it, he'd give me a copy.

While I was sitting there up on the hill thinking about it, I had this urge to grab my flashlight and walk back to the house right then and there and get out the music. But I didn't have the nerve. I lay back down and closed my eyes and played the song in my head, note by note, until I fell asleep.

Holly

11

Will and Ned Brown, and their dad, Steve Brown, arrived to help launch the *Ginny G*. The guys rigged up a big hook and block and tackle so they could hoist her up, and then they lowered her down on a trailer. And then Gigi brought out coffee and muffins. Everyone stood around for a while, talking and joking.

"They don't build boats like this anymore, no sir," Steve said. "Check out the transom, boys, it's made of mahogany."

"Well, by crow, she sure *looks* good," said Ned. "But will she start up? That's the question."

"We'll put Gigi's coffee in her tank instead of gasoline—that'll get her going," Will joked.

Randy helped them hitch the trailer to Steve's truck, and Steve towed the boat down the road to the beach while the rest of us walked down. I didn't want the *Ginny* G in the water. I kept picturing the boat turning... and poor Uncle Jesse in the water... I looked around for Ivy, wondering if she was thinking the same thing. She was walking slowly behind everyone else, her face very pale.

Steve backed the trailer onto the beach and then into the lake until the *Ginny* G floated free. With her three sets of seats and her shiny red waterproof cushions, she almost looked more like a fancy old-fashioned car than a boat.

"Who's going out?" Steve asked.

"I believe it's young Randall's turn to do the honors," said Grandpa.

Randy leaped into the driver's seat, grinning from head to toe. I couldn't believe him. Didn't he care about what Sam had told us?

Grandpa climbed in slowly after Randy and sat beside him. Sam jumped in and squeezed between them.

How could Grandpa or Sam even sit in that boat?

"Let's see if she starts," said Randy. He puts the key in the ignition and turned it.

Sputter. Sputter.

"Pull the choke, pull the choke!" Grandpa shouted.

Sputter. Sputter. Gurgle. Water spat out of the exhaust pipe in the stern.

"She's going, she's going, she's going to go!" Randy shouted. He plunked his hands on the wooden steering wheel.

Aunt Felicity and Aunt Kate climbed into the middle, and Tucker and Tina squeezed in with them. Tucker and Tina weren't thinking about Uncle Jesse, either.

"Now, who wants to ride in the way-back?" asked Aunt Kate. "Holly and Ivy?"

Ivy and I look at each other. "No," we said at the same time.

"Can we?" asked Tigs. The twins usually sat in laps.

"Sure, why not—you're old enough," said Grandpa.

Tigs and Tally jumped into the seat behind the engine hatch.

"I can't believe you guys don't want to go out," said Tigs.

Gigi had been standing quietly behind us. "Since you two girls are available, perhaps I could get you to give me a hand in the new garden I'm making." She circled one arm around Ivy and the other around me. "Could you do that, girls?"

"Yes," Ivy and I both said.

Looking around, Grandpa said, "Where are Sandy and Jake?"

"It's better without them," said Randy with a scowl.

Steve and Will scrambled to untie the motorboat, and *Ginny G* flew off, sending up two plumes of spray on either side.

"She's a beaut," said Ned, turning to me, but I felt cold, as if someone had put ice down my back.

"Come on," said Gigi. We walked with her up the hill and into the woods to a clearing where her and Grandpa's new house was going to be. "Here we are," she said.

We looked at the saplings and blackberry brambles, the fallen trees and branches. "This is going to be a *garden*?" I asked.

Gigi laughed. "Well, maybe more like a sanctuary—I want to put some benches here and have it be a peaceful place for people to come and sit and read or think."

She handed us each a pair of work gloves and clippers. "Cut the saplings as close to the ground as you can, and you can toss them on that pile." Putting on a pair of gloves, she began to clip, haul, and stack. Ivy and I made faces at each other—this didn't look like fun.

We started working. Mosquitoes bit, branches poked, brambles scratched. I could see the window of the studio winking at me through the trees. I wished I could be in the studio painting instead of working.

But this was how it was at Otter Lake. Grandpa and Gigi liked us to have fun, but they also wanted us to help with things. Even Tigs and Tally had to sweep the stone steps down to the lake every morning.

I stopped and watched Gigi working for a moment. She had so much energy. Then I realized with a shock that I didn't think I had ever seen her go out in *Ginny G*. I was about to ask her about it but stopped myself—I didn't want to upset her.

Clip, haul, and stack. As we began to get into a rhythm, the work became a lot easier. Bit by bit we were getting rid of the tangle.

"That's enough for today, girls," said Gigi finally. "I think it's time for some lemonade and cookies."

As we approached the house, we heard voices coming from the porch. The screen door swung open, and Uncle Jake stood in the doorway, his face dark with anger.

"Jake Greenwood!" Aunt Sandy came up to him, shouting. "Something has to give!" Uncle Jake let the door slam with a bang, and as he walked heavily away, Aunt Sandy opened it, yelling, "There you go, walking away again when I'm trying to talk to you!" She stood there for a moment and then let the door slam again before disappearing from our sight.

Ivy pulled off her work gloves and threw them down on the ground. Gigi reached for her, but she ducked and turned and ran into the house.

Gigi took my arm. "All right, Holly, we'll leave her alone for a bit." I helped Gigi make some lemonade and then we sat on the porch with a pitcher of lemonade and a plate of cookies. Piano music came pouring out of the music room.

Gigi listened a moment, and then she said, "I'm glad Ivy has her music. I wish I could think of what to say to make things better for her."

"Me too," I said.

Gigi was raising a cookie to her mouth when she stopped, holding it in midair. "Listen to that!"

I listened, not sure what I was supposed to be listening for, except that Ivy seemed to be playing a new piece, one I hadn't heard her play before.

"There's a Japanese melody woven into that music," said Gigi. "A friend of mine used to sing it. It's...lovely."

I took a breath and plunged in. "Was—was your friend named Kiyoshi?"

Gigi put down the cookie. "How on earth would you know about Kiyoshi?"

There was no going back now. "I found a painting in the studio. It was really pretty—of a pine tree, on the shore by the lake, I think. On the back there was a letter. It was..." I hesitated. I thought I'd better not bring up the trouble that was mentioned in the letter. "It was signed by someone name Kiyoshi, and it was a present for you. It was tucked behind a canvas of *Rainbow* that you painted."

"I remember now," Gigi said softly. She closed her eyes, pressing her fingers against her eyelids. When she opened her eyes again, there were tears in them. "How odd to have this conversation and be listening to that music. Kiyoshi—Kiyo, we mostly called him—was a very dear Japanese boy. And I remember that wonderful painting—so delicate, and yet so particular."

"I can run and get it for you."

Gigi's face lit up for just a moment, but then she shook her head. "Leave it where it is," she said. "Only you and I, and your mother when she's here, spend much time in the studio. It'll be safe there. There are still strong feelings about the Japanese because of the war," she added, as if to explain why the painting should stay tucked away.

"But, Gigi, it's 1965! The war was over a long time ago."

"I suppose if Jake hadn't fought in the Pacific—and if other things hadn't happened—"

"Other things," I said, grabbing at the chance. "What other things?"

Patches of red showed up on Gigi's cheeks. "Holly, you must trust me on this one. Really." She drew her mouth into a straight line, and I knew she wasn't going to talk any more about it. "Are you and Ivy getting along all right?" she asked, changing the subject.

"We're okay."

"I hope you're trying to be a good friend to her."

I gulped. "I'm trying. But it would be easier if she would just stop being so—so—I don't know. She doesn't even want to be in the play this year."

"Well, then," said Gigi, "she shouldn't have to be. It's all for fun, anyhow. Right?"

"But if it's for fun, she shouldn't take it so seriously."

"Hush a moment," Gigi said. "I want to listen—there's the melody again."

She sat very still, her hands folded in her lap. When the music came to an end, she let out a huge sigh. A second later, Ivy started in on the piece she was preparing for the competition.

"The thing is, Holly," said Gigi after a moment, "Ivy can't help taking things seriously. It's just how she's put together."

I headed down the hill toward the lake, stopping for a moment at the Sunbird Tree. I touched one hand to the bird and wished really hard. *Please let things be okay for Ivy.*

No one was down on the dock or the beach. *Ginny G* was still out on the lake. *Rainbow* was pulled up on the beach, turned over. She looked like a large, colorful turtle. I thought about going out rowing, but then I saw Ned chugging toward the dock in his small outboard. He was towing a red sailboat behind him.

Ned grinned and waved as he slowed way down and killed the engine. He coasted in and then leaped from the motorboat onto the dock and secured both boats.

"Is that your brother's boat?" I asked.

"Not likely—Will's is all wood. This baby is fiberglass. Heard tell she's for Ivy and Sam."

"*Really?* Wow! Ivy's going to be thrilled."

Ned looked around. "Meant to be a surprise. Could be I shouldn't have told you. But I've got some papers for the boat I'm supposed to give to someone. I'll give them to you." Ned leaped back into the outboard and rummaged through a box under the bow. "Here you go." He handed me a sheaf of papers. "And Mom wants Gigi to know she's been trying to call her for days—something about the church supper—but your phone is always busy. Is it broken or something?"

"No, it's Aunt Sandy. She's always on the phone."

"Will says sailing lessons start tomorrow."

"Hope you can come sometimes."

Ned's face lit up with a grin again, turning his eyes into half-moons. "Sure hope I can!" Then he said, "Well, I gotta get back. See ya sometime!" He yanked the cord to start the engine. "So long—see ya later," he said with a wave.

I began running a crazy, bouncy, happy run back up the hill. And then there was Ivy, sitting against the Sunbird Tree, and I couldn't stand not showing her the sailboat, so I did.

She almost flipped when she saw it. "Did you wish on the Sunbird for it?" I asked. She laughed and said no. And then the *Ginny G* came in, and of course everyone came over to gawk at the sailboat.

Sam turned to Ivy and muttered, "It's a bribe, you know. To make us not mind going to boarding school. And Dad is going to want you to race it."

"I know," said Ivy, "but I'm not going to."

After supper Ivy disappeared into the music room again. She played the piece she had played earlier. Now I could make out the Japanese melody in it. It made me think of mornings on the lake when the mist rises up in little wisps. It made me think of Kiyoshi's painting.

But I wished she'd stop playing and come out and do something with me. I was bored and restless. The grown-ups were all sitting around reading, and Tina was writing letters to all her friends back home. The twins were sitting at the table, drawing, and Sam and Tucker were outside taking fencing lessons from Peter. I wanted to learn how to fence, too, but I definitely had the feeling that girls weren't allowed.

Mom's voice came loud and clear in my ears. It was what she said every single time I said I was bored. "Find something good to read."

So okay, I started poking around in the bookcase in the living room. I pulled out *Murder on the Orient Express* by Agatha Christie. I was beginning to like mysteries. I opened the book and found a letter tucked inside like a bookmark.

July, 1941

Dear Gigi and Ted,

Thank you for giving us such a nice day at your lovely lake house. We were sorry not to meet your other children, but we were delighted to meet the twins. We are tickled by how different they are—Jake, so shy and serious, and Jesse, so charming and outgoing. Each boy seems to have his own, special set of talents. Jake knows so much about engines, and we really had fun touring the lake with him at the helm of your motorboat. Your Jesse, too, is so knowledgeable. He certainly is up on world events.

And I must say, we were both amazed by your inviting an Oriental foreigner to stay with you! Of course your young man comes from a distinguished family and is attending a fine school of higher learning (Bill, of course, thinks so, as a loyal graduate of Hanford, Class of '22), but it takes confidence on your part to be so hospitable toward the native son of a country that currently is behaving in such questionable ways.

Still, we had a lovely day, and it's rather awful to think we are enjoying swimming and boating and such things while Germany is invading Russia, and the winds of another war are blowing so close to home.

Sadly, our army lacks modern equipment and is filled with men well past retirement age. Bill is afraid they are unfit to fight in a modern war, and everyone knows it's only a matter of time before we're in one again. Your own fine boys are old enough to be called up. Oh, dear—enough of these gloomy matters—our wonderful afternoon spent with you at Otter Lake will be a glowing memory for a long time.

Yrs. affectionately,
Marty and Bill

I stuck the letter in my pocket and looked around the room. Grandpa and Gigi had no idea I was holding a letter that talked about Kiyoshi. Well, I could keep a secret, too.

Ivy's diary

We ate Sunday dinner today outside on the terrace behind the house. Then Miranda, who had a few days off from rehearsing her play, collected the cousins and said, "I'm taking a few liberties with the *Prince and the Pauper*. I'm calling it *The Princess and the Flower Girl*. Tina and Holly will play the main parts. You can guess for yourselves who's going to be the princess and who will be the flower girl."

Tina and Holly started squealing like maniacs.

"Sam, you can run the spotlight when you're not on. Otherwise, you'll be the villain."

"Neat-o," said Sam, happy.

Miranda said, "Tucker will be the hero, Miles Hendon," and Tucker looked proud. "Peter will be the dying king and also the bishop at the end. Tigs and Tally, you'll be the guards. I'll be Mary, Queen of Scots, the jealous sister. Ivy, you will play the musical interludes."

I thought everyone looked at me with pity, as if I were getting a rotten deal. What's strange is that even though I'd told Miranda I didn't want a part, now I had a moment of wishing I did have just a little one. This will be the first summer I don't.

But here's something else strange. I went into the music room, and just like the other day, I played Tōru's composition as my warmup. I like it so much, and it's so relaxing to play it. When I had gone through it once, I still didn't feel like getting down to the Mozart right away. I started thinking about how Gigi was the one who got me into playing the piano in the first place. I opened the piano bench, thinking I'd play some old pieces just for fun, and I found the very first book I'd ever played. I was looking through it when a folded piece of paper fluttered out. I picked it up and read it.

Sept. 15, 1941

Dear Mother,

I have arrived safely in California. My leg is healing nicely. I even did some hiking—good sign—don't you think? I am living at the International House, and I am already making friends. The Japanese I learned from K. has come in handy. Which leads me to say, Could you please find a way of telling him I wanted to say good-bye before I left? I am still so confused about what happened—why did he leave so quickly and never answer my letters?

Love,
Jess

I felt shivery, like a ghost had just walked into the room. And who was K? Then I remembered that at Mrs. LaMare's, Holly had mentioned someone whose name began with the letter K. I jumped up and looked all over for Holly to show her and finally found her up in the Tower Room with Tina. They were practicing the play and didn't even notice me when I came into the room. Holly was prancing around, reading her lines at the top of her lungs. She stopped dead cold when she saw me, and I just stood there like a dummy.

"Do you want something?" Tina asked, hands on hips.

"No, it's nothing," I said. I put the letter in my pocket and went back down to practice. But Mom and Dad were standing in the music room, and they had that fighting look about them. So I backed out of the room and ran straight into Randy, and he said, "Want to go for a drive and a change of scenery?" And I said yes.

Randy drove all around the lake and then halfway up Mount Wigan. We got out of the car and walked around, looking at the view. I felt so much better just getting out of the house, and I suddenly had the nerve to ask Randy what I'd been wanting to ask him for ages.

"Randy, are Mom and Dad going to get a divorce?"

He made a face. "I don't know, but I really don't care if they do at this point. I am so sick of them. This summer is it for me and Otter Lake. And pretty soon the family will be so mad at me, they won't want me around, anyway."

His tone of voice scared me. "Why? What are you going to do?"

"I haven't completely made up my mind yet," he said. Then he reached over and punched me lightly in the arm. "Don't look so worried, Ives."

"Are you going to get shot at or arrested or beaten up?"

Randy ran a hand across his face. "I hope not," he said.

We stayed and watched the sunset and then as we were driving back down the mountain he said, "One thing, though, Ivy. I *am* glad I came back this summer. Because of you. I found someone I can talk to. It really makes a difference knowing you're in my life."

I'm glad I have a diary where I write things down. Because now I have Randy's words forever and ever, and when I feel sad, I'll be able to come to this page and read them over and over again.

Holly

12

Grandpa, Aunt Kate, the twins, Tina, Tucker, and I stood on the dock waiting for Will Brown to come over in his boat. Tigs asked, "Do we get to sail, too?"

"Maybe next summer," said Aunt Kate.

"I knew it," said Tigs sadly.

"We're always too young," said Tally.

We soon could make out a friendly, ruddy face sitting in the stern of the sailboat, and of course it was Will. As he came into the dock and dropped the sails, Tina twirled happily on one foot, and I could picture sitting next to Will in his boat, his hand guiding my hand as I steered.

Will and Grandpa talked about where to put the two boats, and after that was settled, Will said, "Ready for the first lesson?"

Tina, Tucker, and I lined up in front of him on the dock while he stood in his sailboat, keeping his balance with one arm on the boom as he pointed to the parts of the boat. Ivy stood a little to one side looking bored.

"Let's put the sails on now." Will's voice went on and on as he explained rigging. My attention wandered as I wondered if Uncle Jesse had ever learned to sail and if he liked it. Will's deep voice broke into my thoughts. "Want to help Tucker out, Holly?"

Tucker was in Will's sailboat undoing a rope thingy from the mast. I felt myself turning red. This was worse than being caught daydreaming in math class. "Maybe next time," I said lamely.

"I'll try," said Tina.

Then it was my turn. I climbed into the boat and attached the thingy to the top of the sail and put the metal thingies on the track on the mast. I started pulling.

"Sail's twisted," said Will. "Try again."

"You should pay *attention*, Holly," Ivy said.

There wasn't very much wind, so we didn't go out sailing. We practiced rigging and derigging a few more times. I decided that Uncle Jesse would never have liked anything as boring as this.

Out of the blue during supper, Randy said, "Ho Chi Minh says his people are willing to fight for twenty years or more until they win against us."

There was complete silence at the table.

Then Uncle Jake said, "Are you talking about Ho Chi Minh, the communist leader of North Vietnam?"

"Of course I am," said Randy. He began folding and unfolding his napkin.

"And by 'us,' do you mean the United States?"

"You know that's what I'm talking about," said Randy.

Sam jumped in. "Personally, I think all this protest stuff is coming from people who are too wimpy to fight."

Randy threw down the napkin. "That's what people who don't know anything about war always say—"

"I *do* know about war," Sam snapped. "A whole lot more than you do."

"You...will...*not*...discuss...this...at...the...table," said Uncle Jake, each word dropping out of his mouth like a stone.

I looked up at the beams over my head.

"Where do we discuss it, then?" asked Randy. "In your sailboat? Swimming in the lake? While our government kills Third World people on the other side of the world?"

I noticed there were a lot of cobwebs up in the beams.

"You're always spouting propaganda," said Sam.

Uncle Jake pushed back the bench, leaving the table.

Grandpa's voice shook as he said, really quietly, "I, for one, would like to enjoy strawberry shortcake without voices being raised."

I brought my gaze down from the beams and stared at him. My heart twisted. An old person looking sad is the saddest thing in the world.

Randy began to push himself up from the table, too.

"You know that my father, your great-grandfather, was the owner of one of the mills in Manchester, Randy," said Grandpa.

Randy slowly sat back down. "Yes, I know that the Greenwood money comes from the mills."

Grandpa didn't say anything for a moment, and then he continued,

"When I was a boy, the workers went on strike, protesting the working conditions. And then one night they came and stood outside our house shouting about the unfair conditions at the mill. They hurled rocks and smashed our windows. I was only ten, and I was terrified. I was also confused. I wondered then if my father was a bad man. But I also knew this about him. That he had come over to this country as a boy without a penny to his name. I knew that he had worked his way up to the top from nothing. And I also knew that he was a good provider for his family and that he was a kind father."

Randy frowned and pulled on his beard.

Grandpa lifted a trembling hand and rubbed it across his face. "My father eventually negotiated with the men, and conditions improved for them. But two conflicting things happened to me that night. I developed a distaste for violence and also an understanding of the need for it. I saw the desperation and the anger that drive men to hurl rocks at the windows of a grand brick house, but I also understood that my father's background had driven him to work hard to be successful, sometimes without mercy for others. Fortunately, in his case, he was able to do the decent thing. But things are always more complicated than they might first appear, Randy. There are always at least two sides to every story."

Everyone at the table was still.

"It's a lesson, Randy, that I haven't always managed to remember. So I'm just asking you not to repeat some of the mistakes I've made. Don't let anger at injustice prevent you from seeing where another person—I think there's an expression young people use nowadays—might be coming from." He paused and then said, "The Greenwoods have always had a tendency to flare up in anger. I've worked my entire life to keep my temper in check, sometimes successfully and sometimes not. But if you can manage it, the life of those around you will be the better for it."

Randy bowed his head, staring straight down at the dessert in front of him.

"And now," said Grandpa, "whoever is closest to the whipped cream, could you please pass it to me?"

"Tally and I made the whipped cream," said Tigs in a small voice.

"I love your whipped cream, girls," said Grandpa with a smile.

Everyone at the table started talking at once, everyone except for Gigi, who was wiping her eyes with a napkin.

After supper Ned came over to give Gigi a message from his mother, and Tucker said he wanted to play Kick the Can. I was It first, and I found Tigs and Tally and Tina, and I put them in jail, and then Sam came and kicked the can and freed them. It took me forever to catch everyone after that, and then Sam agreed to be It. As it grew dark, I crouched behind the barn, pretending I was in World War II hiding from the Nazis. Pretending was still fun when it was just me and no one else knew what I was doing.

I heard rustling in the woods behind me, and then a twig crackled. I lay flat on the ground, trying to blend into the dirt and the leaves. And then a body sank down beside me.

"Hi," it said in a whisper.

It was Ned. Our elbows were touching. I could hardly breathe. At least if we were caught, we'd be caught together.

The wind was whipping across the lake. When both sailboats were rigged, the sails flapped furiously.

Now Ivy skipped around on the dock. "This is my favorite sailing weather," she said. "This is sooo great."

"Sure you know what you're doing, now?" Will asked her as she untied her boat. After a few days of lessons, Will had decided to make Ivy his assistant, a smart move on his part.

"Of course," she said, tossing her head.

"Of course," said Tina, imitating Ivy's tone of voice.

"Come out with Tuck and me," Ivy said to me.

"Oh no you don't, we get Holly," said Will.

Will wanted *me* to come out with *him*. As I climbed into his boat, he said, "Tina, you take the tiller first, and I'll sit up here beside you. And you can sit on the other side, Holly."

The other side was the Side of Doom. It was the side that tilted into the lake. And every few seconds, a stream of cold spray leaked down inside the neck of my Windbreaker. I squeezed my eyes shut, trying to shut out the sensation of tipping.

Will and Tina started talking about popular music. "Bob Dylan, blah blah, James Brown, blah blah, the Temptations, blabbety blah."

"Ready about." I heard Will's voice. "You're going to have to move to the other side, Holly."

Move? But I was numb with cold and fear. I couldn't move.

"Holly, *move!*" Tina screamed. "You're in the way!"

I opened my eyes and ordered my numb self to move across the centerboard trunk while Will and Tina yapped about the Lovin' Spoonful. As far as they were concerned, I didn't exist. Will only wanted me in the boat as extra weight.

A gust of wind roared at the boat. The lake starting pouring in on my side. I screamed and scrambled over the centerboard trunk, knocking my ankle bone against it. Tina laughed out loud.

"Steady now," Will said to Tina. His hand covered hers as he brought the boat back to a steadier course. Somehow, Tina had managed to get the starring role in *my* daydream.

"It's your turn now, Holly," said Will.

"It's okay, I don't have to," I said, trying to sound casual.

"No, you should," said Will, smiling at me earnestly. "Your parents are paying for your lessons. I wouldn't feel right not giving you a turn."

I inched my way back to the stern and gripped the tiller with both hands.

"Easy there, girl!" Will said, grinning.

His teeth were very white. I should have been glad I was making Will smile. And now, finally, here I was sitting next to him up on the good side of the boat, the Side of Glory. But Tina was sitting up there, too, as close to Will as she could get. Wait a minute, why wasn't *she* sitting down on the Side of Doom?

Will said, "We better come about. We're getting close to the shore."

Which way did the tiller go? I was too embarrassed to ask. I guessed wildly and pulled the tiller toward me. The boom whipped over, and the boat lurched wildly. As we took in half the lake, I let go of the tiller. Tina started screaming.

Will scrabbled across me, pushing me out of the way as he grabbed the tiller. The water we had shipped sloshed around above our ankles.

"Start bailing," Will ordered as he tossed me the bailing bucket. He didn't say it nicely.

"I'm sorry," I said. "I got confused."

"Coming about and jibing," said Will shortly. "We need to go over that."

When it was time to come in, Tina made the dock landing.

"Perfect," Will said.

When Ivy and Tucker came back, their faces were shining. The two of them kept laughing as they derigged the boat.

"See you later, Ivy, that was really fun," said Tucker. "Can't wait to go out with you again."

When our boat was derigged, I sloshed my way up to the house in my soaking shorts and sneakers. Gigi was sitting on the porch painting a vase of snapdragons.

She looked up. "My, you're soaked, Holly—I guess it's windy out there. It must have been fun."

I didn't say anything.

"There's a letter for you from your mother," she said, nodding to the table in front of her.

I scooped up the letter and went into the house to change into dry clothes. Sam and Peter were at the table with math books and papers piled up around them. Aunt Sandy hadn't been able to find a math tutor for Sam, so Peter had offered to help him. I noticed a sheet of paper covered with drawings of flags under Sam's elbow. "That's math?" I asked.

Sam grinned. "Each time I finish a page of problems correctly, I get to draw a flag. These are all the enemy flags of World War Two. That's the German national flag," he said, pointing to a swastika inside a circle. "This is Fascist Italy. This is imperial Japan."

"I like the Japanese flag," I said, looking at the big red circle. "It's pretty."

"Yeah, pretty, like blood is pretty," said Sam.

"What's this one?" I pointed to another red sun with red rays coming out of it. It reminded me of the sun in the Sunbird.

"That's the Japanese rising sun flag. The Japanese navy used it during the war," said Sam.

"You look soaked," said Peter. "Sailing must have been fun."

I mumbled something and ran up to the Tower Room and changed, and then I climbed up on my bed and read Mom's letter.

Dear Holly,

I'm wondering what is making you ask about Uncle Jesse. It's a curious coincidence because one of the reasons I decided to join Dad this summer in California was so I could conduct some research concerning Jesse. It's a long story, and I want to tell you properly, and not in a letter. I promise I'll tell you all about it when we get to Otter Lake. Until then, please keep the reason for my research to yourself.

And then she went on about other things, and asked all sorts of questions about what I was doing. I lay on my back, staring up at the rabbit-deer knot. It would be better, I thought, to be a hawk than a rabbit. Then I could swoop over the whole world and look down and see all the secrets and finally understand them.

Ivy's diary

The wind was great for sailing this afternoon. I said, "Hey, Hol, let's go out in my boat. We can just sail—it won't be a lesson or anything." She said, "No, I can't, Tina and I are learning our lines."

I can tell she doesn't really like the lessons—she just wants to moon around Will. She still doesn't even know how to rig a boat. I notice she gets out of rigging every time.

I said, "You wouldn't be scared of sailing if you actually learned how to do it."

She said, "You wouldn't be scared of acting if you actually did it."

Holly never used to argue so much.

Today Dad came down to the dock and asked Will if he would crew for him in the next weekend race. Will said it would be an honor. Dad said, "That's wonderful because I can't seem to get anyone in my family to feel that way."

I was sitting in my boat coiling up lines when Dad said that. I know he meant me to hear him, and I was sure he was about to start bugging me about racing, but—here's the surprising part—he didn't. And then I suddenly wanted to say, "I'll crew for you," because I thought I'd learn a lot about sailing from him, and the pressure to win would not be on me. But I just couldn't get the words out.

And then he and Will started talking about boatbuilding. Dad gets along so much better with Will than he does with Randy. And then the aunts came down with lunch, and while everyone was sitting on the dock eating, Dad started asking Will questions about his future. Will said he might enlist in the navy.

Randy started tugging on his beard, and then he said, "Really?" with this edge to his voice. Then he added, "If you enlist in the navy, you'll end up in Vietnam. Why would you do that?"

Will said, "I can go to college on the GI Bill. Otherwise, I can't afford to go. And also because I think it's the patriotic thing to do."

Randy started to open his mouth to say something, but Gigi reached out and put a hand on his arm. Randy took a breath and closed his mouth. I think he was remembering what Grandpa said at the table the other night. Sam didn't say anything, but he sat there glaring at Randy. I know Sam is all gung ho for war, but somehow I can never take him seriously. He secretly still plays with G.I. Joe toys.

Tina was sitting next to Will. Tigs and Tally started teasing her. "Is Will your boyfriend?" Tigs asked. Tina turned bright red and said, "No way." And Tally said, "Then how come I saw him kissing you?" And Tina turned even redder and said, "Shut up, Tally, you did not, and stop being a brat." But Tigs and Tally laughed their heads off.

Randy and Will used to be good friends. I hate how they act around each other now. And I can't picture Will Brown carrying a gun and killing people. All he knows about is boats and making jokes and flirting with girls.

Later I heard Aunt Felicity say to Gigi, "That Will Brown is a very charming boy, but he needs to be careful. Tina's head over heels, but I don't see him being that serious about her."

Gigi said, "His future is up in the air. I think he's confused about what's in store for him. There's this Vietnam business—I don't know whether or not to call it a war—but whatever it is, it's going to make things hard on young men."

Her saying that made me remember the letter of Uncle Jesse's I had found. I still wanted Holly to see it, but when I went to look for it, I found it in the shorts I had worn when I was out sailing. It had gotten soaked and soggy, and I couldn't read it anymore.

Holly
13

It was a dead-flat-calm day on the lake. No sailing lesson today, and anyway, Ivy and Sam were about to go off looking at boarding schools.

Ivy refused to eat breakfast. She sat at the table looking not one shred like herself in a skirt and blouse. Sam was eating, but he had refused to put on the sport jacket Aunt Sandy had bought him to wear for his interviews. He was wearing an ancient jacket and tie, and the jacket was too big and looked funny and old-fashioned on him. I was pretty sure it was the one Uncle Jesse was wearing in the photograph marked *Jesse on his Save the Otter Campaign.*

Tina fell over laughing when she saw Sam. "Professor Samuel Greenwood, I presume."

"Grow up, will you?" said Sam.

Aunt Sandy was dressed up in a suit and high heels. Her hair was poufy, and she had on her raccoon makeup. "You're trying to sabotage this, Sam," she said angrily.

Sam scowled and dug his hands deep into the pockets of the jacket.

"Come on, we need to get going," said Aunt Sandy, looking at her watch. "Ivy, take your hair out of that ponytail. You look older and more sophisticated when it's free."

"I don't want to look older and more sophisticated," said Ivy, hunching her shoulders.

"*Uma Cotcha Walla,*" I said under my breath.

"That's not going to help," she said.

Seeing Sam in the jacket reminded me that Miranda had told us to start thinking about costumes for the play. I went up to the second floor and walked down the hall to the little room at the end where all the walls were lined with tin sheets so the mice couldn't get in and chew up the old clothes and linens and blankets that were stored there. I pulled the string over my head that turned on the light and just stood there for a minute, loving the smell of mothballs and the odd, old things up on the shelves.

There was the dented bugle my great-grandfather had played in the Civil War, and the Russian samovar tea set that had been a gift from one of Grandpa's students. Among all the knickknacks and the old dresses and coats and army uniforms and hats, we never had any trouble finding props and costumes.

I found an old green-and-yellow apron that I thought would be perfect for the Flower Girl. I put it on and tied the strings at the back. It was long on me, but I thought that would be good. Slipping my hands down into the pockets, I discovered a scrap of paper with a recipe scribbled on it and an old newspaper clipping.

Son of Tokyo War Lord Has Haven in New Hampshire, I read.

The article was dated September 23, 1943, and it said that while New Hampshire boys were dying in Japanese prison camps, a wealthy Japanese boy was able to live an easy life as a student at Hanford College. A lady who was interviewed said, "We ought to make chop suey of him." Another lady whose son had starved to death in a Japanese camp said, "I wouldn't want him around. I have no use for Japs. We are too lenient with them, give them too much liberty."

I felt sick. I closed the trunk where I had found the apron and ran up to my room and climbed up on the bunk and took out the sketchbook, which I was keeping safe under the blanket on the end of my bed.

I pulled out the photographs of Jake and Jesse and Kiyoshi. He must have been the "wealthy Japanese boy." Grandpa must have taught him at Hanford. I wished I could ask Grandpa about him. I wondered if there was still time to write Mom and ask her. She was getting back in about a week. A week! That wasn't long. I could wait until I saw her.

I studied the photograph. Mom and Dad and I often played a game on long car rides where you thought of people you knew and compared them to other things.

Jake was like black, bold capital letters. Jesse was old-fashioned script in light blue ink.

Jake was an oak. Jesse, a birch.

Jake was a truck. Jesse, a bicycle.

Kiyoshi was a bird. His eyes were bright, and his shoulders were bony.

And then I noticed something I hadn't really zeroed in on before. Uncle Jesse was holding a carved box in his hands. I thought it looked familiar. I tried to think of where I'd seen it before, and then I remembered it had been in the bottom of the trunk along with the photos.

I climbed down from the bunk and went into the storage closet. I knelt down by the trunk and opened it up. The wooden box was still at the very bottom under everything. I pulled it out and rested it on the trunk. The initials JG were carved into the top.

JG were the initials of all the Greenwood kids—John, Jimmy, Jake, Jesse, Jenny—but Jesse was the one holding the box in the photograph. Now in the daylight I was able to pry the lid off the box.

One by one I took out: a small rock. A slab of black mica. A blue jay's feather. An otter carved out of wood. It was lying on its back with its paws curled on its tummy.

There was a medal with faded ribbons saying For Excellence on the Debating Team.

There was also a black-and-white pen-and-ink drawing of Otter Lake House, signed by Gigi with a note saying, For my darling Jesse.

A folded sheet of green paper turned out to be a hand-lettered program.

THE GREENWOOD PLAYERS PRESENT:
The Prince and the Pauper...
Adapted and Directed by John Greenwood
Jesse Greenwood as the Prince
Jake Greenwood as the Pauper

My other uncles and Mom were in the play, too, and I recognized the names of a lot of second cousins and local people like Steve Brown.

And finally there was a small leather-bound book. It said Diary on the outside in gold letters. The first page said, This diary belongs to Jesse Greenwood. The pages smelled musty, and only about ten pages at the beginning had writing on them.

I began to fight with myself. It was a diary. But Uncle Jesse wasn't alive anymore. So it wouldn't hurt him if I read it, would it?

I tucked the box under my arm and backed out into the room. I took off the apron and hung it over the back of a chair and then stuffed the sketchbook and Jesse's treasure box into my knapsack. In about a minute

I was down at the beach pulling *Rainbow* into the lake, hoping like mad that Tucker or Tigs and Tally wouldn't see me and want to come with me.

A rowboat is great. You just climb in and row. No sails to put up. No lines getting tangled.

I rowed along the shore until I came to Secret Cove.

Uncle Jesse's bobbing handwriting reminded me of a fleet of sailboats racing along on a windy day.

> June 26, 1939
>
> I am sitting in Secret Cove thinking about how all my life I have been afraid of so many things. I have to start facing my fears.
>
> I used to be afraid to walk down the dark hall between my room and the bathroom. I used to be afraid of spiders, especially of those huge, hairy ones that lurk about under the dock. I know they aren't tarantulas or anything, but that's always what they make me think of.

I laughed. Just like me, Uncle Jesse was afraid of the spiders under the dock.

> But now I am afraid of two things that seem more important than the dark or spiders.
>
> The first thing is: competing.
>
> I am afraid to do well at the things I'm good at because I am afraid of making Jake feel bad. We grew up with everything always being fair and even-steven. If we poured a glass of root beer, the glasses had to be filled exactly to the same point.
>
> The thing is, I am good in school—it comes easily to me. School is harder for Jake. This whole year, I haven't wanted to use my brains the way I could have because I haven't wanted to outdo Jake. I joined the debating team, but I never told anyone I won a prize.
>
> The second thing: how people react when I stick up for what I believe in.
>
> Last summer the McCloskey boys were chasing otters and ducks and loons in their speedboats. I hated them for doing that. I dressed up in my best jacket and went and sat on Hutchings' porch for a month. I stopped people who came in and asked them if they wanted to start a society to protect the wildlife on Otter Lake. About two hundred people signed, and one of them was our state senator,

who lives on the lake. And now, this summer, it is against the law to chase wildlife on any open body of water. Anyone caught will be fined $100.

Well, things got better for the otters but worse for me. The McCloskey boys saw me out fishing in *Rainbow* the other night and started zooming their motorboats around and around me, cutting it really close. I thought they were going to smash into me. I took on a lot of water and was pretty much swamped. It makes me afraid to go out on the lake.

June 27, 1939

I am sitting in Secret Cove and thinking about how to face my fears.

When I was younger, I made myself walk really, really slowly down the dark hallway. Nothing happened to me—I wasn't attacked by monsters, so ever after I have not been as afraid of the dark except when my imagination gets the better of me. I realize it is my own imagination that manufactures fearful things. I decided I could also do something about the spiders. The next time we were at the lake, I made myself hang my head over the edge of the dock and look underneath it because that is where the spiders live. I counted to one hundred. The spiders didn't attack me.

So now, it's the same thing. I can't be afraid of those boys. I can't let them stop me from going out in my own boat. I just hope the McCloskey brothers don't run me over and drown me.

Now I am sitting in Secret Cove again. The McCloskey brothers came out after me again. The same thing happened—their motorboat came really close. They yelled insults at me. But *Rainbow* and I are still here.

Two more days of being razzed. Each time I think I'm going to be a goner.

Nothing today.

Three days have gone by and no McCloskey boys. Maybe they can't afford to buy all the gasoline it takes to swamp a rowboat. Or maybe they got tired of the sport.

There were a lot of blank pages, and then there was another entry.

Jake is working with Steve at Brown's Marina this summer. He works on the engines people bring in for repairs. Pa and I came by the marina the other day. Steve's dad, Willard, said, "I never met a boy as bright as your Jake. He's got a problem solved before I can even think of it. You ought to be real proud. I'm sure you're plenty bright, too, Jesse, didn't mean to say you aren't—"

Made me laugh. All this time I've been afraid to be smarter than Jake, and it turns out he's really just as smart, if not more so. We're just different, is all. It actually wasn't very smart of me not to figure that out earlier.

And that was it for the diary. I wished Uncle Jesse had written more. What little I learned about him from his diary I liked so much.

I put everything back in the box and closed it up. I was sitting on a fallen tree trunk a little way up from the stream that led into the cove. I got out my sketchbook and started sketching *Rainbow*. I was just putting the finishing touches on the sketch when I heard the snapping of twigs—and there was Uncle Jake.

Holly

14

"Ha," said Uncle Jake. "It's you." He came and sat down on the trunk beside me. "Seems as if I'm always finding you here."

I didn't like people looking at my drawings. I wanted to hide it from him, but at the same time I was afraid of seeming rude. I sat without moving a muscle, feeling awkward.

"You've got your mother and your grandmother's artistic eye," he said. Then he added, "I miss your mother. When is she getting here?"

"Pretty soon," I said. "About a week."

"Teaching out in California, huh?"

"Yup," I said.

"Your mother and I became chums just before I got shipped off to war. I could talk to her in a way I couldn't talk to other people. And she always had the knack of knowing just what to say to me. I'll be glad to see her." He cleared his throat slightly. "You look just like her, you know— when she was your age."

Uncle Jake's saying that made me happy. I thought Mom was really pretty. And it made me think, if he had a soft spot for Mom, the softness maybe carried over to me and explained why he was overall nice to me.

But as he was talking, I was slowly trying to close the sketchbook, and one of the photos I'd tucked into it slipped out. Uncle Jake reached down to pick it up, and then rested it in the palm of one of his big hands. It was the picture of Jesse in the jacket. Uncle Jake studied it for the longest time. I held my breath, waiting for him to explode, but he just sat there, staring and staring.

He finally said, "I remember when this photograph was taken. It was for the newspaper, when my brother went on a campaign to rescue the otters that were being chased by motorboats. Me, I was all set to go and punch the lights out of those guys. Not Mr. Pacifist, though, oh no. Where did you get this photograph, anyway? And what are you doing with it?"

"I—found it in a trunk in the storage closet in the Tower Room," I said.

"Snooping about, eh?"

"I didn't mean to be snooping. But I am curious about—please don't get mad at me, Uncle Jake—but I am curious about Uncle Jesse." My heart was jittering a mile a minute. "Please tell me about him."

Uncle Jake groaned and put his head in his hands. Then he said, "My brother was—Oh, he was..." He seemed to fizzle out.

"He was good at debating," I said.

Uncle Jake took his head out of his hands and looked at me strangely. "How did you know that?"

"He was good at a lot of things."

"Yes, well, I guess you could say I spent half my life trying to keep up with my brother. He was better-looking, more sociable, smart—the girls all liked him—"

"He faced his fears," I said.

"What on earth would make you say such a thing?"

I reached down and picked up the box and took out the diary and handed it to Uncle Jake. He slowly opened the book and started to read. I sat, waiting, listening to the breeze swish through the tops of the trees. I thought how strange it was that Uncle Jesse had written these words so long ago right here in this cove, and now Uncle Jake was sitting here reading them.

"Ha," he said finally. He wiped his eyes with the back of his hand. "Guess he figured out smarts come in all kinds of flavors." He didn't look at me, and his voice was tight. He lifted the rock out of the box. "See these little red bumps? They're garnets. And this black mica. Came from the mica mine."

"Did Uncle Jesse carve this otter?" I asked, reaching for it. I was about to hand it to Uncle Jake, but he jerked his hand away.

"I never thought to see *that* again." His face darkened and he didn't say anything more.

"I'm s-sorry," I stammered. "I don't understand."

As I turned the otter nervously over and over in my hands, I noticed two tiny markings on its belly. "That looks like Japanese writing," I said. And then I knew. "Kiyoshi carved it!"

Uncle Jake shifted away from me, his face darkening even more. "How do you know about him?"

I found the photograph of Jesse standing with Kiyoshi on the dock and handed it to him.

"Well, I'll be damned!"

I felt a rising panic. "Don't be mad, Uncle Jake. Please don't be mad at me!"

"Mad?" Uncle Jake turned toward me in amazement. He sucked in his breath and seemed to hold it forever, and then he let it out in one long sigh. "You're afraid of me. I thought you were the spunky one in the family."

"I only get scared of you when you get mad," I said in a small voice.

"Listen here, Hollis Greenwood Swanson, I am *not* angry at you right now."

"You sound like you are."

Uncle Jake leaned his elbows on his knees and, resting his chin in his hands, stared out at the lake. "I guess I can get angry all I want, but anger doesn't bring him back."

He let go of Jesse's photograph and it floated to the ground. I leaned forward to pick it up. *Ask him*, a voice in my head seemed to be urging me. *Ask him to tell you about Kiyoshi.*

I held the photograph in one hand and the otter in the other. "Uncle Jake, please tell me why Kiyoshi was here in New Hampshire—and please don't yell at me—"

"Stop it, Holly," said Uncle Jake. "I'm not going to yell at you. I just don't know exactly where to begin." He placed his hands on his knees, curling and uncurling his fingers. "Your grandfather was teaching at Hanford," he said finally. "Kiyoshi was his student. He was the only Japanese boy in the entire school. And the reason he was there had to do with events that took place years before Kiyoshi was even born. For a very long time, Japan had been isolated from the rest of the world, but in the eighteen hundreds, the country decided to open up and expand its knowledge outside its boundaries. One way of doing this was for the wealthy Japanese families to educate their sons in the United States. Kiyoshi's grandfather went to Harvard. Later when he married and had a family, he planned on sending *his* son to Harvard, too, until he came to New Hampshire in 1905 as part of a diplomatic team that negotiated a peace treaty between Russia and Japan."

"They came here to New Hampshire?"

Uncle Jake smiled. "Don't sound so surprised. Yes. Right here in New Hampshire. In Portsmouth. Don't they teach you anything in school? It was called the Peace Treaty of Portsmouth. It was brokered by Theodore Roosevelt. Old Teddy won the Nobel Peace Prize for it. Well, Kiyoshi's grandfather met some professors from Hanford on that occasion. They showed him the college. Convinced him that a small school could be just as good as a big university. He liked the countryside here, so he decided to send his son to Hanford instead of Harvard. The son, and that was Kiyoshi's father, was the first Japanese student ever to graduate from Hanford. He enjoyed the experience so much, he decided to send *his* son there."

"And that was Kiyoshi," I said.

Uncle Jake nodded.

"Okay, so Grandpa was his professor."

Uncle Jake nodded again. "Yes, he was. And at home Pa often talked about the shy Japanese student in his class. Gigi already felt sorry for him. She was sure the poor boy must have been terribly homesick, and then when she learned that he couldn't get home for summer vacations—it was too far to go back and forth—she suggested he spend a few weeks with us here at the lake. Dad wasn't sure it was a good idea—he didn't want to get involved in the life of a Japanese boy, especially with the increasing tensions between Japan and the United States. But Gigi insisted."

Out on the lake an outboard buzzed by, its bow slapping against the waves. I knew it was Ned, and I wished he were here, sitting beside me, listening to Uncle Jake with me. I didn't like being alone, hearing this stuff.

Uncle Jake shifted slightly on the tree trunk. "The two of them—Jess and Kiyo—took to each other. That was hard for me. When we were youngsters, Jess and I were like you and Ivy—we did everything together."

Like Ivy and I *used* to be, I wanted to say. Uncle Jake took the photograph from me and studied it again.

"When Kiyo came into our lives, it was right when things were changing between Jess and me. Jess liked books. I liked using my hands.

Eventually he figured out he wanted to be a writer—maybe a journalist—and I knew I wanted to be an engineer. But we didn't know back then that you could have different interests and still get along."

Something shifted and lightened inside me. I realized that was exactly what was happening to Ivy and me.

Uncle Jake rubbed his hands together. "Back then I only knew one thing. And that was, I missed my brother. Growing up, he had been my best friend. And now he was spending all the time I had left with him before we went our separate ways with this stranger—a *foreigner*." He allowed the photograph to slip between his fingers and drop into the open box that was sitting by his feet. "Kids in town began to notice—called us Jap lovers. Can't say I blamed them for it—at the time, those Japs weren't doing us any favors."

I winced at the way Uncle Jake said "Japs."

"But they can't *all* have been bad. And Kiyo—what did *he* have to do with it?"

Uncle Jake scowled. "Look, I lost a lot of good buddies in the Pacific. I can't ever pretend to have any love for the Japs—Japanese." He curled his fingers into fists. "But we weren't at war yet at the time, and I stuck up for Jesse. Got into a few scraps with the townies."

I looked down at the photograph of Uncle Jesse and Kiyo. I noticed the *Ginny G*'s bow in the bottom left-hand corner.

Ask about what happened in the Ginny G. The words sprang into my mind and sat on the tip of my tongue.

But Uncle Jake turned to me and said, "Okay, changing the subject now. How is the sailing going?"

"I *hate* it!" I yelled so loudly, we both jumped. "I am just plain scared stiff every time I go out in the boat. And I don't understand any of it—heading up, heading down, coming about and—and *hard to lee*—what the heck is *that*?"

Uncle Jake put back his head and laughed more loudly than I had ever heard him laugh. "Time to face your fears, missy," he said.

Ask him, ask him now, while he's laughing.

"Uncle Jake, what happened with you and Jesse in the *Ginny G*?"

Uncle Jake jerked his head back as if he'd been stung. "Don't know what you've heard, but whatever you've heard is probably not the truth, and the truth—well, what's the point of that anymore?" He stood up. "Meantime, face your fears."

I watched as he walked heavily away. I held the otter, turning it over and over again. I wished it could talk—or did I? I put it back inside the box and closed the lid. Maybe that was where secrets were safest—in a box with the lid closed.

Ivy's diary

Back from looking at schools. Two boys' schools, one all girls, and one coed.

It was hard to tell what the schools were like because mostly there weren't that many people around, except at one place where summer school was going on. They all seemed the same to me. They were either made up of big brick buildings with ivy on them or of old-fashioned white houses. Lots of athletic fields. Lots of famous people who had been students. Every single person who showed us around said, "You get individualized attention here." All the schools had dining rooms where the students ate "family style."

The first time someone said "family style," Sam whispered to me, "If it's like our family, that means a lot of arguing at the dinner table."

Cornish Hall, the coed school, had this humongous auditorium and little practice rooms. The admissions person said Cornish Hall was famous for its music.

Mom said, "Isn't this exciting!" But I found it intimidating. What if I end up going to one of these hotshot places and everyone is way better at playing music than I am? Who says I can get in? I have good grades and all, but I have the impression you have to be a genius to get accepted.

I forgot to say that Dad refused to go with us today. He said he didn't want us to go away to school, and if Mom wanted us to go so badly, she could just take us around by herself. Mom was furious, and she drove the car so fast we were actually too early for the first interview. Sam finally went into the headmaster's office, and when he came out he was grinning his head off.

While we were being shown around at the next school, Sam pulled me aside and told me he'd acted as dumb as possible during the interview. He said that was going to be his strategy in all his interviews.

I didn't try to act dumb in mine, but I think I was. I know my voice came out way too soft. One lady kept telling me to speak up.

Summer classes were going on at the last school we looked at. This one history class was meeting outside, and the teacher was talking about World War II. Sam couldn't help it. When the teacher started asking questions, Sam answered them. Even when the class ended, the teacher and Sam got to talking more and more, and the teacher asked, "How do you know so much?" Sam told him the name of some of the books he's been reading. The man clapped his hand on Sam's shoulder and said, "I'm very impressed." Then he told us his name—Mr. Huff—and that he teaches history in the summer, but that he is also head of the school. And he told Sam he was admitted to the school on the spot.

Sam said, "But I'm a terrible student."

Mr. Huff said, "Not anymore," and then he said he has a jacket cut just like Sam's, and he hopes Sam will bring it to school with him because he'll look so distinguished in it.

I had this moment of being jealous of Sam. He got into a school, just like that. I guess because Sam gets bad grades, I secretly thought he might not be that smart.

I have to admit I look at Sam differently now.

Holly
15

When I woke up in the morning, I heard the wind in the pine trees.

"Great sailing day!" Ivy said, leaping out of bed.

I pulled the covers over my head, trying to shut out the sound.

"Come on, Holly, you're going out with me in my boat."

"I'm not going out."

Ivy reached up and pulled the covers off me.

When we got down to the dock, Tina said, "Golly! I've never seen so much wind!"

"Enough to blow your pretty hair into your pretty eyes," Will teased.

Tina batted her eyelashes. Tucker pantomimed throwing up.

"Holly is coming out with me today," said Ivy.

I waited for Will to protest, to say, "No, Holly must come out with *me*," but he simply said, "Good idea—we'll switch things around a bit. Hop in, Tuck."

Tucker looked a little disappointed, but he followed orders. I didn't have time to be disappointed. Ivy stuffed the sails of her boat into my arms. "Today is the day you are learning how to sail," she said in a school-teacher tone of voice.

Ivy made me spread the sail out on the dock. She showed me where each point of the sail was attached, and for the first time I understood what to do.

But once we pushed off from the dock, I immediately felt overwhelmed.

"Will and Tina always sail," I said. "I just go along for the ride."

"I know," said Ivy. "That's why you're going out with me today. Pull in the jib sheet and don't let it luff." The wrinkles in the small sail smoothed out as I pulled it in.

And then we were rushing along. My heart dropped into my stomach.

"It's kind of gusty," Ivy said in a pleased voice. She sat up on the Side of Glory, leaning way out, staring up at the sails, steering the boat with one foot.

"Ivy! Is it okay to steer like that?"

"Of course. You don't need to worry, Hol. Come sit up here with me. Jam the jib sheet into that cleat if you don't want to hold on to it."

I moved up to the Side of Glory. I felt better, although a sheet of spray smacked me in the face.

Ivy laughed. "This is the greatest!"

I tried to breathe deeply to make my heart slide back to where it belonged.

Another gust of wind set Ivy laughing again. "There we go, good wind. Pull the jib in, Hol," she said, squinting up at the sails.

The boat heeled way over and another sheet of spray hit me full force and dripped down inside my Windbreaker.

"This is exactly perfect, you and me out in a sailboat, right, Holly? Let's come about. Ready about, hard to lee."

The boat hung for a moment in the teeth of the wind and shook all over. The shore seemed scarily close. "Back the sail," said Ivy calmly. "Hold the jib so it fills backward—and I'll move the tiller in the opposite direction, and presto—" We shot away from the shore. "Now pull the jib in from the other side."

Sailing with Ivy was much better than sailing with Will and Tina. I wished I'd gone out with her long before this.

"Now it's your turn."

"What?"

Ivy laughed. "How else are you going to learn? Come on, we're changing places. Don't worry—I'll be sitting right here next to you. I'll control the main until you feel more comfortable."

I scrambled past Ivy, and then there I was, gripping the tiller with both hands.

"Pick a point to steer for—Big Tree or something. You'll steer straight if you keep your eyes glued to where you're going."

I squinted at Big Tree. An extra gust of wind skittered down the lake. The boat heeled sharply.

"Eyes on Big Tree," Ivy reminded me. "And eyes on the lake, too. And on the sails. Actually, you have to look everywhere. And you only need to use one hand on the tiller," she continued. "And you have to keep a light hand on it."

I relaxed my grip, kept my eyes on Big Tree—and I was sailing. I looked up at the sails. They were sparkling white, and the lake was sparkling, too, with stars of light dancing on the black waves.

And then we saw Will's boat just ahead of us.

"Let's be pirates," said Ivy. "We'll sail close to the shore and jump out and board 'em when they least expect it. Mind if I take over?"

Her eyes were shining as she took the tiller again. As the bow headed up closer to the wind, the boat heeled again. We sailed as close to the shore as we could.

"Do you think they can see us?" I whispered, but of course they could.

"Hey!" Tucker shouted.

Ivy came about, and soon we were sailing so close to Will's boat I could lean out and touch it. Tina was skippering, and Tucker, sitting closer to the bow, was drenched.

"Isn't this fun?" Tina asked, a dazzling smile on her face.

"F-fun," Tucker joked through chattering teeth.

"I'll race you to the dock, Ivy," said Tina.

Ivy shook her head.

"Oh, come on, Ivy," said Tucker.

"Ivy's afraid I'll beat her," said Tina.

"Come on, Ivy, let's do it," I said.

Ivy's mouth tightened. "I don't race," she said.

"I'll treat whoever wins to an ice cream sundae," said Will.

"Ivy?" I asked. "*Please?*" I wanted Ivy to show everyone how good she was.

"Okay, we'll come about, and then when we're side by side, running with the wind, we'll start," said Ivy. Her face was a blank. Not a good sign. "Ready about, Holly," she said without any expression.

With a fluttering of sails, we changed direction. Tina followed suit, and soon we were sailing side by side, both heading toward the dock.

"One, two, three, go!" Will and Tucker yelled at the same time.

"Okay, here you go, Holly," said Ivy. She let go of the tiller. "It's all yours." She moved past me.

"*What?*" Without a skipper, the boat began to swing up into the wind.

"You're the one who wants to race," she said coldly.

"What's going on? Holly's going to race?" There was laughing and jeering from the other boat.

I gripped the tiller, tears springing into my eyes. But I didn't have time to feel sorry for myself. My eyes ran up the hill above the dock for something to sail for. I saw the Sunbird Tree.

"Eyes on the tree, eyes on the tree," I muttered to myself.

Ivy wasn't holding the main anymore. She wasn't holding on to anything. I had to lean way out to grab the mainsheet.

"Careful not to jibe," Will warned from the other boat. "If the jib flips over to the other side, you could jibe any second."

Now you're teaching me, I thought bitterly.

I reached forward and grabbed the jib sheet and tugged it until the sail filled. But while I was doing that, the boat headed up and the mainsail started luffing like crazy.

Eyes on the tree, I muttered as I headed back down, *and please don't let us jibe.*

Another gust sent us plowing forward. Tina's boat surged forward, too. There was so much pressure on the rudder, I had to keep the tiller steady with both hands while keeping hold of the mainsheet and the jib. Will's boat was so close I could hear the creaking of his mast. Tucker was chanting, "Go, Tina, go!" I narrowed my focus so I could see only my jib and the tree.

Tina's boat was ahead of me, approaching the dock. Tina made a neat dock landing, and everyone cheered.

And then I, too, was headed, at a very fast rate, for the dock.

"What do I do?" I screamed. "Ivy! Come on! I've never made a dock landing."

The dock, and Will's boat next to it, were coming closer and closer. Ivy didn't say a word.

"Start heading up!" Will shouted from the dock. "Push the tiller away from you; *push,* as hard as you can! And let go of the sails!"

I pushed and then let go of the tiller and the sails. Everything swirled about me. I buried my head in my hands.

And then suddenly the world was still.

"Oh, good dock landing!"

I forced myself to look up. Will Brown was standing on the dock, holding on to the mast of our boat. His head was thrown back, and he was laughing.

"Congratulations! You just made your first, successful dock landing. I think you deserve a sundae for this."

"But I won! I won!" Tina shouted, dancing on the dock.

"You should have seen the expression on your face as you were coming in," said Tucker. He was doubled over with laughter.

They were all laughing—everyone but Ivy.

"Why did you do that?" I yelled at her. "I could have crashed!"

Ivy turned away.

"You always just sit there and don't say anything, and you act like you're the only one in the world who has feelings!"

Ivy climbed out of the boat without a word and disappeared up the hill.

Holly
16

Will and Tina helped me derig Ivy's boat.

"What's up with Ivy?" asked Will.

Tina made a face. "She's just so *special*," she said meanly.

I walked miserably up the hill, stopping at the Sunbird Tree. I slumped against the trunk and stared down at the holes in my sneakers. I thought that if Ivy had been out rowing *Rainbow* this morning instead of sailing, we would still be friends. But no, it wasn't sailing that made us fight. It was me. I was a coward. I thought about Uncle Jesse. It was time to face my fears.

Tucker was coming up the hill. I got up and grabbed him by the arm. "Just so you know," I said. "I'm going out."

He looked startled. "What are you talking about?"

"I'm going out sailing."

Tucker shook the hair out of his eyes. "Don't you know how windy it is out there?"

"That's why I'm going out."

"I don't feel like getting soaking wet again."

"Not you—me."

"You're going by yourself?"

I was afraid of losing my nerve. "Do me a favor—go up the hill and grab me a sweatshirt and something waterproof while I rig the boat again." Tucker made a face. "Please."

Tucker grunted, but he headed up the hill as I headed down to the lake.

The sails were hanging in the boathouse rafters, drying from the morning's sail. I hauled them down and carried them into Ivy's boat. At least I knew how to rig a sailboat by myself now.

"Holy halyards!" Tucker exclaimed as he came down onto the dock. He was carrying a sweatshirt and a Windbreaker. He tossed them into the boat. "Think it's windy enough? It's much windier than it was even an hour ago." He watched me attach the jib. "I could go out with you."

I wanted Tucker to come out with me so much, I almost started crying. "This is something I have to do by myself."

"I didn't even think you liked to sail," he said.

I didn't answer. I was trying to tie a figure-eight knot in the end of the jib sheet.

"That's a six, not an eight," Tucker said. He crouched on the edge of the dock and fixed the knot for me. "I don't think they're going to like it—"

"Who?"

"You know—Grandpa and Gigi. They won't like you doing this."

I put on the sweatshirt and the Windbreaker and a life jacket. "Okay, I'm ready."

"I'll cast you off," said Tucker.

"Thanks, Tuck," I said, moving back to the stern. I held the mainsheet between my teeth and grabbed the tiller with both hands.

Tucker pushed the boat off from the dock with his foot. The sails caught the wind immediately. As I tugged in the mainsail, the boat heeled sharply. The lake poured in over the side with a sickening, *whooshing* sound.

"Let out the sail!" Tucker yelled.

As I let out the sail, I scrambled up the side like a mountaineer clawing for a secure hold. The boat flattened so quickly, I was almost pitched over the side.

"You can't beat me, wind," I said, my eyes filling with tears. I jerked the tiller and pulled in the sail again. The boat heeled sharply again, and for some reason, I couldn't steer. The boat kept slipping sideways.

Out of the corner of my eye, I could see Tucker jumping up and down on the dock, waving his arms and yelling. And then it dawned on me why I was tipping so easily and I couldn't steer. I had forgotten to put down the centerboard. I reached forward and released the centerboard, and it slid down with a thud. I took a breath and picked Big Tree as my focus. I pitched on the waves, and every now and then a sheet of water smacked in over the bow. Climbing up on the Side of Glory, I leaned out.

"As long as it doesn't get any worse than this, it'll be okay," I said to myself.

But it was gusty, a hurricane one minute, a wimpy little breeze the next—and then all at once, the sound of the wind in the trees startled me. I had been concentrating so hard, I hadn't noticed the approaching shore. I had to come about, but which way did the tiller go? Why didn't I know this by now?

The rocks under the water loomed like sharks. I had to act. "Ready about!" I commanded myself, and pushed the tiller.

The sails flapped, and the boat was caught in the teeth of the wind. I leaned forward and grabbed the jib so it filled backward. I reached back and yanked the tiller over the opposite way. "Go, boat, go!" I yelled. A fresh gust roared over the boat, and I scrambled up just in time and leaned out.

The open lake was before me now.

"I'm doing it, Uncle Jesse!" I shouted. "I'm sailing!"

"I don't know if I'd call it sailing," I answered for him. "More like surviving."

"That was a neat trick with the jib," I said.

"Ivy's a good teacher," I said in a deeper voice.

"She's a good sailor." (My voice.) "I bet she could beat Uncle Jake in a race."

"She won't race." (Jesse's voice.)

"If I could sail like she does, I'd be out there every weekend, beating the pants off all those hotshot sailors."

I started to laugh. I wasn't mad at Ivy anymore. When I came back in, I'd go and find her and make her talk to me.

I tugged in the sail, and with a burst of confidence, edged the bow a little closer to the wind. And that was when the gust hit me. In a split second, I took in half the lake. And it didn't stop. I stared in disbelief as the Side of Doom slid farther and farther into the lake.

"We're capsizing!" I said to the invisible Jesse. Just as the sails struck the water, I slipped and lost my grip, and then everything was cold and wet and dark and quiet.

Ivy's diary

I'm upstairs in the Tower Room. They rang the bell for lunch. I don't
want to go.

I'm sitting up on Holly's bed, on the top bunk. It's so different
from my bunk. Like being in a tree house instead of a cave. Hol and
I used to pretend the bunks were boats. We couldn't touch the floor
or we'd be eaten by alligators. On rainy days we'd hang blankets
down and make a clubhouse.

I don't really know why I came up here—just a place to sit and
write, I guess, or maybe I'm trying to see what Holly sees, staring
at the knots Holly looks at every night. They're different from the
knots I look at. Oops—I just knocked a box off her bed.

Wow. I jumped down to pick it up and all these things were
scattered all over the floor. There are some neat things, like an otter
carved out of wood and all these photos.

I figured out the box belonged to Uncle Jesse. And for the first
time he's real to me. I think he looks like Randy before Randy grew
a beard. I can see Sam in him, too—maybe in the shape of his ears?
Mine, too. Everyone's always saying we have elf ears. Uncle Jesse
had them, too! There's a picture of Uncle Jesse standing with someone named Kiyoshi. I think he must be Japanese because Tōru Kameda's son's name is Kiyo.

I hear someone coming up the stairs—

It was Tucker coming to tell me it was lunchtime and they were
looking for me. I told him I wasn't going to lunch. I can't stand the
thought of sitting at the table with Tina. And Will Brown will probably be there, too—he always is nowadays. I am so sick of him.

Tucker asked, "What am I supposed to tell them?"

I said, "Whatever you want." Then I felt bad because what happened today out in the sailboat isn't Tuck's fault.

He said, "I like sailing with you better than Will and Tina."

I said, "Thanks, Tuck, and just tell them I'm not hungry, but that I'm okay. Okay?"

"Holly's out—" Tucker started to say, but I said, "I don't want to talk about Holly right now, okay?"

Tucker shook the hair out of his eyes and opened his mouth to say something else.

I said, "I mean it, Tucker."

He kind of screwed up his face, but he didn't say anything more, and he went downstairs.

I just read Uncle Jesse's diary. He talks about being afraid to compete. Is that my problem? Am I afraid of competition? Being better at things than other people?

I actually think it's the opposite. I want to win at things so badly I'm afraid to lose. Maybe that's why I was such a jerk to Holly in the sailboat. I couldn't stand the thought of Tina beating me to the dock and then lording it over me for the rest of the summer.

Holly
17

It's so dark and quiet, I don't have to worry about the wind anymore—but I couldn't breathe and my chest hurt. Splinters of pain were shooting into my lungs. I pushed away at the dark and the cold, and finally—I burst up into bright, dazzling light. Gasping, I closed my eyes.

The sun burned inside my closed eyelids. It was a red disc with rays of light shafting out of it—a Japanese sun. When I finally opened my eyes, I saw a head bobbing in the water just to the right of the sails—an otter? Oh no, it was the bailing bucket, floating away—

I burst out laughing. I was laughing so hard, I had to put my head back so I wouldn't swallow half the lake. "I can't believe this," I said out loud, and it was comforting to hear my own voice.

Slowly my mind began to wake up. A few days ago, Will had given us a capsize demonstration. I tried to think about what he had said. First I had to get myself untangled from the lines, and then I had to get the sails down.

It was hard to tell which line was attached to what, but I finally managed to pull down both the main and the jib and stuff them into the boat. Then, hand over hand, I pulled myself around to the other side. Scrambling up onto the blade of the centerboard, I reached up for the gunwale and leaned back. As the mast slowly rose up, water sloshed out of the sails. Just for a moment the boat sat upright, but almost instantly it tipped back over in my direction.

I flopped my way back over to the other side and stood on the centerboard again. The mast slowly rose again. "Stay!" I ordered, but without someone on the other side to balance the weight, I couldn't keep the boat from tipping again. "Tim-*ber*," I said as the mast fell like a tree.

Now what?

I looked around. I didn't see any other boats on the lake. No one else was stupid enough to be out in wind like this. I splashed my way around the boat one more time. My body felt so weighed down by my wet clothes, and I was so tired. I rested my head on the centerboard.

Had anyone even noticed I was out? Had Tucker told them?

And that was when I heard the rumble of the engine. I looked up and saw the gleam of a varnished bow heading straight for me. Uncle Jake was at the wheel of the Ginny G, and Will and Tucker were beside him.

It occurred to me I was going to get into trouble. I took one look at Uncle Jake's face; his expression was a lot scarier than any old windy day. I decided not to look at him again.

I heard a splash, and there was Tucker swimming toward me. "Stand on the centerboard," he called out. "I'll hang on to the other side." He was grinning. All the fear and all the tiredness instantly melted. I could do anything now. One more heave, and the mast came up, and with me on one side and Tucker on the other, we were able to keep the boat stable.

"I'm throwing you a line," Will yelled from the stern of the Ginny G. He seemed very serious, and I didn't want to look at him, either. "Make it fast to your mast."

Soon enough, Ginny G was chugging slowly toward home, pulling us with her. Tucker and I sat far back in the stern, the tiller between us. I felt light-headed and giddy with relief. "Thanks for coming to rescue me."

"You were doing okay until you went over."

"You were watching?"

"Well, it was lunchtime, and you didn't show up, so I told everyone you had gone out. I wasn't sure if you wanted me to tell or not, but since you weren't in yet, I thought I should, so everyone jumped up from the table and came rushing down to the dock. Grandpa was all for going out and getting you right away, but Uncle Jake said no. He said you were trying to face your fears."

"He *said* that?"

"He got the Ginny G out and brought her alongside the dock and sat in her, watching you through the binoculars. Even after you capsized, he said, 'She's going to be all right. She can handle herself.'"

Tucker seemed so matter-of-fact about it all, it made me laugh. And I *was* sailing along pretty well until I capsized. Even then, I'd *handled* myself. I started singing.

"I love to go a-capsizing
On the ocean blue
And as I go a-capsizing
I sing this happy tune."

Tucker joined in.

"Cap-size-ing! Cap-size-ing!
Ca-ah-ah-ahaha ap-size-ing
All on the ocean blue!"

"You know what?" Tucker said, breaking off suddenly. "Uncle Jake's driving *Ginny G.* I've never even seen him in the motorboat before."

"I know," I said.

When we were almost in, Tucker untied us from the motorboat.

"Get this boat bailed out and put back together," Uncle Jake barked, "and then we'll meet you up at the house."

"You don't have to help me with this," I said to Tucker as we coasted in toward the beach.

"I have nothing better to do," he said. For once, his hair was plastered to his forehead so I could see his eyes. They were brown with green flecks in them. It wouldn't be long before girls decided Tucker was cute.

"You think this is fun," I said.

He grinned. "It is."

It took us a long time to get all the water out of the boat, untangle the lines, and put everything in order. Not that I was in a hurry. I wanted to put off going up to the house as long as I could.

As we were working, Tina and Sam came down to the beach. "Grandpa wants you to meet him on the porch as soon as you finish here," said Tina. "Am I ever glad it's not me in trouble."

Tucker gave her a sour look. "I'd like to see *you* go out in wind like this by yourself."

"I'm not crazy," said Tina.

"What was it like to capsize?" asked Sam.

"Not so bad," I said. "Except for getting stuck under the sails."

Tucker and I sponged the last drop of water up from the boat. Then as I slowly trudged my way up the hill, the full force of what I had done hit me.

Grandpa had only ever yelled at me once—the time when I asked him why he didn't want to look at a photograph of Uncle Jesse. That was before I even knew I had another uncle. Now I thought about him drowning in the lake, of course Grandpa would be upset that I'd gone out in a sailboat on the windiest day ever.

Everyone was on the porch waiting for me—everyone who mattered, that is—Grandpa and Gigi, Uncle Jake, Will—

"What were you thinking?" Grandpa asked. The sadness on his face made me want to go and crawl into a dark corner.

I took a breath and clenched my fists. I thought about how to explain myself. "I was so scared every time I went out sailing," I said finally. "I wanted to make myself go out on a windy day, so I would have to get over my fear. I was—I was—trying to face my fears."

Uncle Jake glanced at me quickly and then looked away.

"And I was thinking so much about doing that, I didn't think—I didn't think about worrying anyone. I'm sorry if I worried you—" I stopped, not wanting to break down.

Grandpa's face relaxed. "So what you did—was an act of courage." He reached out and pulled me to his side.

"Courage or insanity," said Will. There was just a flicker of a smile on his face. I could feel the tension on the porch relax.

"Winston Churchill said, 'Courage is rightly esteemed the first of human qualities, because it is the quality that guarantees all others,'" said Grandpa. He held me tight.

I could hardly believe it. I was expecting to get into the worst trouble of my life, and here Grandpa was quoting Winston Churchill. And then I remembered that Grandpa had gotten a medal for bravery for defending a bridge in World War I. Being brave mattered to him.

Tucker walked onto the porch. "You should have seen it," he said. "The waves were ten feet tall, and Holly was attacked by sharks, and she kept saying, '*It's okay, I can do this.*'"

Everyone started laughing.

"I promise I won't go out sailing on the windiest day ever again," I said leaning into Grandpa.

"Just let someone know if you do," said Grandpa. "Your mother and father are arriving at the end of the week, and they'll want to find you here."

I nodded, gulping back a sob. I wanted Mom and Dad to be here now. I wished they'd never gone to California in the first place. Whatever it was Mom was looking for—was it really so important she had to leave me behind?

And then I couldn't wait to go and find Ivy and tell her I wasn't afraid of sailing anymore.

"You're still wet," she said as I came up into the Tower Room. "Didn't you even change your clothes for lunch?" She was sitting up on my bed.

"I didn't go to lunch, which you'd know if you'd been there yourself."

And then I saw the box and the otter and Jesse's diary next to her. "What are you *doing*?"

Ivy slid down from the bunk bed. "I'm sorry," she said. "I'm sorry I've been so—so—I don't know—the way I am. You don't have to like sailing, Holly. You can do whatever you want to your hair, and you can like boys, and—"

"Ivy—stop—"

But Ivy burst into tears. "Everything's been—so—the piano competition—Mom and Dad—and boarding school—and you—but Uncle Jesse—" She started laughing, even though the tears were streaming down her face. "I read his diary. It helped me understand some things about myself."

Tucker clumped up into the Tower Room. "Gigi says you both have to come down and eat something—" He stopped and stared at Ivy. "Oops, didn't mean to butt in."

Tina was next. "Oops—sorry—didn't mean to break up the pity party—"

"Did Holly tell you?" Tucker asked.

Ivy wiped her face with the back of her arm. "Tell me what?"

"I haven't even had a chance to," I said.

"Holly went out sailing by herself," said Tucker, "and she capsized and she—"

I grabbed a dry T-shirt and some shorts and went into the bathroom to change. I sat on the edge of the bathtub and waited. I could hear Tucker's voice going on and on. When it was quiet, I came out. Both Tucker and Tina had left. Ivy stood staring at me, eyes wide.

"Did you really go out?"

I nodded. "I was facing my fears. I—"

"Like Uncle Jesse," said Ivy. After a moment she said, "I hope you don't mind that I read his diary."

"It's not *my* diary."

"You were really brave!"

"I was really dumb!"

We both laughed.

"Let's go eat something," said Ivy. "I'm starving. And guess what? I'm going to face my fears, too. I'm racing this coming weekend, and you better crew for me!"

Holly
18

The races were held in the open part of the lake with Mount Wigan watching over everything.

Ivy was quiet and serious the whole time we sailed around the course, and we came in third. I was thrilled when we crossed the finish line two boat lengths ahead of the boat behind us. But Ivy was mad at herself.

"That's *good* for your very first race," I kept saying as we sailed home.

"I like winning," she said with a sigh. Then she said, "I'm really confused by something. You know how Grandpa always comes out in the *Ginny G* to watch the weekend races and cheers Dad on and everything?" I nodded and she went on. "Well, you know how I asked him not to come this time because it was my first race, and I didn't want him watching me?" I nodded again. "Well, it got me thinking. He *loves* the *Ginny G*, Holly. I mean, she's his baby. I don't know why it didn't occur to me before, but if Sam's story about what happened to Uncle Jesse is true, I don't think he would love her as much as he does."

"*Ginny G* and Grandpa go together," I said slowly, thinking about it. "They're kind of the same—two old boats." Ivy smiled slightly, tugging at her ponytail. "And maybe Grandpa wouldn't hate *Ginny G* even if that happened. Maybe he thinks it wasn't *Ginny G*'s fault but the fault of whoever was *driving* her that day."

Ivy and I both stared at each other. I think it was the first time either of us had even thought about who might have been at the wheel.

"Do you think it could have been Dad?" she asked in a small voice.

I looked down at the little bubbles in the varnish of the floorboards. "Maybe Grandpa *wouldn't* blame whoever it was," I said, trying to reassure her. "You heard how he says he knows there's always more than one side to every story."

Ivy shook her head. "Yeah, I know, but Randy told me later that Grandpa saying that made him mad. Because if you're always trying to be fair by seeing both sides, you can talk yourself out of trying to change bad things."

She looked up at the sails and moved the tiller a fraction of an inch toward her.

"Maybe, though, they were just both horsing around, so it was both their faults."

We heard the whine of Ned's outboard. He slowed down to a putter and yelled, "Hey, Hol, are you going to the church supper next Sunday?"

"Yeah!" I yelled back.

"There's a dance afterward," he said. "Want to go with me?"

"Sure!" I yelled again. I felt the color rush into my face, and I didn't dare look at Ivy.

"That's one thing I'm not ever going to win at," said Ivy as the whine of the outboard faded. "Going to dances," she added, as if I might not understand.

In the afternoon Gigi asked us to keep Mrs. LaMare company while she went shopping for her.

As always, Mrs. LaMare brought out her stamp collection. She turned the pages, showing us the American stamps first and then the ones from other countries. When we finished with those, she turned to the back where she kept the covers.

This time the envelopes startled me.

The handwriting on them looked just like Uncle Jesse's handwriting. I picked one up from the top of the pile. It was addressed to Mrs. LaMare and the return address in the upper left-hand corner said *Blk. 34 Bldg. 13, Apt. 4, Manzanar, California*, and it was postmarked *Manzanar, Calif. Dec 21, 1942*. The two-cent stamp was red, and the words *Army and Navy* were printed above a cannon, with *For Defense* beneath it. Two cents! Right now in 1965 stamps were a nickel!

"Is there a letter inside?" I asked Mrs. LaMare. "Okay to look?"

"Why, yes, these are historical artifacts," said Mrs. LaMare. "It's good for young people to learn history through old letters."

Ivy was sitting next to me, looking over my shoulder, and her eyes widened as I pulled out a folded piece of paper. She moved her chair closer to mine and we both started reading.

December, 1941

Dear Mother,

This letter is written in haste—I have left college. Of course I am worried about how Pa will take this news. I know he is already disappointed with the turn my life has taken—my last-minute decision not to go to Hanford, for one.

Mother, I want you to know that before I was injured, I was planning on becoming a conscientious objector. Only Jake knows this—I never had the courage to tell you and Pa. Any time I ever tried to broach the subject of pacifism with Pa, he became angry. As it turns out, the Army wouldn't take me now anyway because of my leg.

But Mother, please understand it was never my intention to sit by and watch other people suffer. I have a terrible need to be useful, and the most useful thing I can think of doing right now is helping the Japanese families here who are being herded like cattle into relocation camps. (They are called "camps," but they are really blocks of barracks surrounded by barbed wire.)

I am living in one now, and my friend, Reiko, and I are going to teach the children because now more than ever they need to keep going to school. Mother, please don't be upset with me. The reason our soldiers are going overseas is to fight against hatred and prejudice. Please see that I am also trying to fight against prejudice right here in our own homeland.

Much love,
Jess

I felt a shiver go all through me as the conversation between Randy and Gigi in the car that morning after church came back to me. "Mrs. LaMare, these letters were written to my grandmother," I said. "Why do you have them?"

The blue in Mrs. LaMare's old eyes seemed to deepen as she struggled to remember. "Gigi gave the letters to me. She thought I'd like to have the covers for my collection."

I looked at the envelopes again. "But, Mrs. LaMare, they were sent to you at *your* address."

Mrs. LaMare shook her head. "It seemed—I seem to remember it was a good idea."

"Look," said Ivy. She held up another envelope. "Here's one with different handwriting, and it's postmarked from Glover. No return address, though."

The writing was sloped to the right. It was round and childish-looking. I had seen that handwriting before, too. Ivy pulled the letter out of the envelope.

December, 1941

Dear Mrs. Greenwood-san,

Now that war has been declared, my father wants me to come home. I certainly understand the reasons for this, but I would prefer to stay here. I am happy here, happier than I have ever been. I feel as if I can breathe more freely in the air of your country, as imperfect as it might be. I am not foolish enough to believe any people is perfect, and there are those here who look at me and say, "You are Japanese, why don't you have buck teeth? I thought all you Japs had buck teeth?" Only Americans are free enough to speak with such rudeness!

I am wondering if wanting to stay here in college in the United States is an offense against my father's will? But as the son of the enemy, my presence here must also be an offense to the authorities of the college.

I wish I could speak of such weighty matters with someone who understands me, as you have always seemed to do. But I do not wish to burden you in these matters. I have already burdened you enough.

Your friend,
Kiyoshi

"Kiyoshi!" Ivy exclaimed. "He's the one!"

"You knew about him?"

"No. I—" We heard Gigi come into the house. As she poked her head into the room, both Ivy and I froze. "Girls, I'm going to take a little longer today to clean out Mrs. LaMare's refrigerator."

"That's fine, Gigi," I said, trying to keep my voice steady. "We're having a good time."

As soon as she left, Ivy whispered, "A little while ago I found a letter

Uncle Jesse had written mentioning a person whose name began with K. I kept meaning to tell you about it, but come on, let's read as many of these as we can before Gigi makes us leave."

December, 1941

Dear Mrs. Greenwood-san,

Your letter to me saying I must follow my own conscience and not be ruled by political considerations, or even by my sense of duty to my family, was a great comfort to me. And then it turns out the need to make a decision is out of my hands. I will not be able to get to San Francisco before the last boat home makes its departure—and so my father and the president of the college say I am to stay here for the duration of the war. It is my Fate. I cannot pretend to be sad about this.

Yours with deepest gratitude,
Kiyoshi

December, 1941

Dear Mother,

I only have a moment, but can you tell me what is happening to Kiyo? I pray that Dad will speak to the president of the college and urge him to stand up for him. Oh, Mother, I would do anything to be home in New Hampshire right now.

With all my love,
J.

January, 1942

Dear Mother,

This "camp" was thrown together so quickly, it is not a fit place for people to live. The barracks are so small, there is no privacy for anyone. The wind is always blowing, and sand is constantly sifting into the cracks so everything is covered with a gray film. On some blocks, the food is passable; on others, it is terrible. The children are all sick from the typhoid shots they have been given. Reiko and I are trying to organize a school, but there are no supplies. To begin with, I have been reading aloud to them from Kipling's "Just So" stories. They seem to like these stories very much, and they are comforting to me as well. I am instantly transported back to being six years old, with Jake and me sitting on either side of Pa while he reads to us before bedtime. (A friend has smuggled this letter out with him to mail it from the "outside." Otherwise, I am sure it would be censored.)

All my love,

J.

March, 1942

Mother,

There is trouble and unrest here at the camp. It is cold, and the wind blows all the time. It is not the wind I have always loved—the wind that sent pine needles swirling or the waves on the lake dancing. I remember waking in the Tower Room and hearing the brushing of the pines across the sky, and I would instantly feel glad to be alive. Here the wind makes a constant and incessant wailing sound—it makes me think of a little boy who cannot be consoled. I think sometimes it is the earth itself grieving over this conflict.

But it is the kids here who give me hope. There is a ten-year-old boy in my "class" who is so intelligent, so eager to learn. (I say "class," but there is no organized school as yet.) What impresses me most is how adaptable the people are. They are angry at what has happened to them, but they also say, "We are here, so we must make the best of it." I know Pa would admire this attitude. I remember going on camping trips, and it would be raining, and he would always say, "We can't let a little rain spoil our fun." Must go.

Love,

J.

March, 1942

Dear Mrs. Greenwood-san,

I often think my family is like your family. I, too, come from a family of five children. But the males in my family are all expected to go into business. When I come of age, I must sign a contract saying I shall devote my life to furthering the financial gain of my family.

Do you know what my dearest wish is, Mrs. Greenwood? Someday I would like to run a school in the countryside of Japan and teach Japanese children all the things your children learned at Otter Lake House—to be at home in the water and on the water. To love the woods and the mountains. To paint the sunsets. To play games with each other. Nature would be their teacher. As a career, this would definitely not be acceptable to my father, but what do you think, Mrs. Greenwood?

It is only to you that I confide such thoughts. And I wonder how you and I can remain friends under such circumstances, where our countries are at war with each other. Your sons will soon be fighting my brothers and my cousins. What a sad thought—I can hardly bear thinking of it, Mrs. Greenwood. I will tell you the truth: I count you as my true friend and more of a mother to me than my own mother, and Jesse more as my true brother.

Your friend,
Kiyo

May, 1942

Dear Mother,

The poor people here at the camp do not understand what has happened to them—why they are being treated like animals. There is not enough food to go around, not enough charcoal to keep people warm. I do what I can, but there is growing distrust of Caucasians here. They say the white guards are stealing sugar and meat from the warehouses and selling it on the black market. I am glad at least that I am working with the children. The kids do not care what color I am, and they sincerely want to learn. They miss being in school. This is what keeps me going. I always thought I wanted to be a writer or a journalist, but I have discovered I have an aptitude for teaching. I hope someday the Old Man will be pleased to hear I want to follow in his footsteps. I know that right now he does not want to know anything about me.

But please send a hello to anyone you think might like to hear from me—if there is anyone. I would like to write to Jake but do not know where he is at present. I assume he has enlisted. It worries me to think of him as a soldier. He might seem like a tough guy, but in truth, he is actually much sweeter and softer than I am. Please give Jenny a hug from me and greetings to Jimmy and John. AND a big thank you to Mrs. LaMare for being our intermediary. And please, please tell Kiyo I am thinking of him.

Love,
J.

"Intermediary," I said slowly. I turned to Ivy. "What does that mean?"

"Someone who's in the middle," she said. She frowned, thinking, and then said, "They must have decided it was safer to send their letters to her than to Otter Lake House. Because of Grandpa."

"I guess," I said, but still there were things I didn't understand. There was the matter of the great sorrow that Kiyoshi had brought to the family. I began to put the envelopes back into the stamp album. "Thanks, Mrs. LaMare," I said, "that was really interesting."

"I want you to have these letters, Jenny," said Mrs. LaMare, pressing them on me. "They belong to you." And because I saw Gigi coming toward us, I took them.

As soon as we got home, I ran with Ivy out to the studio. I showed her Kiyoshi's painting of the pine tree and the letter he had written on the other side.

"I love his painting," she said.

"Me too," I said. "I wish it didn't have to be hidden away."

"I found a letter, too," she said. "I kept meaning to show it to you, but then it got wrecked when I went out sailing. It was from Uncle Jesse saying he'd made it to California and his leg was healing. And he mentioned something about K. and how he didn't get to say good-bye to him. Something really bad must have happened."

"Where did you find that letter?" I asked.

"It was tucked into one of Gigi's old music books in the piano bench. It's like Uncle Jesse keeps leaving clues, like he *wants* us to know about him."

I wrapped my arms around my knees and hugged them to my chest. "That's *exactly* how I've been feeling all along!" Then I told Ivy about the conversation I'd had with her dad when he found me reading Uncle Jesse's diary in Secret Cove—how he'd told me how jealous he was of Kiyoshi.

Ivy looked alarmed. "Did you ask him what happened in the motorboat?"

"I started to, but he got really upset."

For a moment I was sure she'd flare up at me in the old way. She opened her mouth and then closed it. Then she said, "Yeah. I bet."

Without saying anything else for a while, we sat staring at Kiyoshi's painting.

"Someone at Hanford College might know where he is," said Ivy suddenly. "Kiyoshi, I mean."

"We could call the college and ask," I said, scrambling to my feet.

We ran into the house and looked up the number of the college, and then we stuffed ourselves into the little telephone closet. Ivy dialed, but she made me do the talking.

"Hanford College," a lady answered.

"Good afternoon," I said. I read from a piece of paper where we'd written out what I was going to say. "I am calling to inquire if you have a person there who's in charge of knowing about people who used to go the college?"

"A director of alumni—why, of course we do—that's Mr. Pollard," said the woman. She had an oldish voice. "I'm sorry to say, however, that Mr. Pollard is on vacation." There was a pause, and then she said, "Perhaps I can help you? I have been with the college a long time now. Are you inquiring about a recent graduate?"

"No," I said. "He went to Hanford during World War Two. He was Japanese—"

"You must mean Kiyoshi Mori," said the lady. "I happen to know he passed away—fairly recently, in February, I believe—"

"Oh, no!"

Ivy raised her eyebrows at me.

"Oh, dear, was he a friend of yours?"

"He was—a friend of the family's," I said.

"I'm so sorry you had to find out in this way," said the lady, "and he was so young, too, leaving behind a wife and two children. Imagine being the only Japanese boy on campus when Pearl Harbor was bombed! President Clemens brought him into the office and told him the college would look after him for the duration. Now, *that's* something for the college to be proud of, don't you think?"

"Yes," I said faintly, and added, "Thank you for your help," and I hung up.

I sagged against the door of the closet. "He died," I said, my eyes filling.

"It's so strange," said Ivy, her eyes filling, too. "Crying for someone we've never even met."

Holly
19

Gigi had all of us cleaning up Otter Lake House. She wanted to spruce things up for Mom and Dad, who were arriving late in the evening. We raked and swept and washed and mopped and dusted and baked and picked flowers. The twins made a big WELCOME HOME sign.

Because of all the chores, it was almost dark by the time we sat down at the table for supper. Aunt Felicity lit the candles, and the whole room seemed to glow.

Tigs started the meal by saying, "I made up a joke today. Does anyone want to hear my joke?"

Tucker said, "No," but Gigi said, "Of course we do."

"When is a boat not a boat?" Tigs burst out, barely able to contain herself. "When it's ahead, like in a race. But also like a *head*," she said, pointing to her own head.

"I have a joke, too," said Tally, but before she could tell it, Ivy said, "Did we have to drop the bombs to end the war?"

Everyone stared at her. It was so unusual for her to bring up *any* topic at the table, much less war and bombs. But Randy was quick to give her an answer. "No," he said, his face furrowing into the familiar look of anger he had so often these days.

"Yes," said Sam, almost before Randy finished. "Thousands more people would have died if we hadn't done that."

"I don't understand," said Ivy. "Does that make it right? Didn't thousands of people die from the bombing?"

"Ivy!" Randy exclaimed. "I don't believe it! Someone in this family is finally asking questions. But while we're on the subject of right and wrong—" He paused for a moment, gulping slightly, and then he said, "This seems to be a good moment to announce that I'm leaving school. I'm going to work full-time for the civil rights movement, and if I get drafted, I'm—I'm going to burn my draft card." Randy was shaking slightly, staring defiantly into the candle flames.

Sam said, "Speaking of dropping bombs, you just dropped a big one, Randy."

Randy lifted his chin. "I've decided I'm going to speak openly about my decisions and not hide things."

Uncle Jake's face flushed red, and then his fist came down on the table. He started to roar. Tally started crying. Tigs put her hands over her ears. I was sandwiched between Aunt Kate and Sam. I slid down and turned around and dove through the gap beneath the backboard of the bench and the seat. I started to run, knocking my shin against a chair, and hurled myself out of the room and onto the porch. I pushed open the screen door and let it slam behind me. I ran down the stone steps and didn't stop running until I got to the Sunbird Tree.

I leaned my head against the trunk. I could still hear angry voices drifting down from the house. I touched the Sunbird. *Please, please let the war in this family stop.*

I wanted Mom and Dad.

Then I kept running, hoping that down on the dock I'd be out of range of the yelling.

The moon was rising. Silver and gold circles of light shimmered on the black waves. It was quiet and peaceful.

I drifted into the boathouse. A bat fluttered out of the rafters. Tina always screamed at the sight of bats, but Ivy and I were proud of the fact that we weren't afraid of them. Waves lapped gently against *Ginny G*'s hull as she floated in her stall. I walked over to the far side of the boathouse where she was tied up. She was sitting there so harmlessly. I jumped into the stern, and the cool of the plastic cushions felt good against my skin.

"Hol?"

Ivy's light, musical voice called from just outside the boathouse door.

"I'm in here."

Ivy came into the boathouse. "Where are you?"

"Here—in the motorboat."

"You're in the *Ginny G*?"

"Remember how we used to bring our stuffed animals down and sit in the boat and play?"

"Yeah, it was sort of cozy—our own world."

"Are they all still yelling up there?"

Moonlight shone in through the boathouse windows, lighting up Ivy's face. She gave an unhappy, jerky nod of her head. "Everyone got up from the table except for Dad and Randy. Even Sam and Mom stayed out of the fight this time."

Ivy sat down on the edge of the stall and let her feet dangle for a moment, and then she jumped into the stern next to me. Her being there felt so familiar. I wished we were six years old again.

"I feel so sorry for Randy," Ivy said. "I can't help being on his side. It isn't easy to stand up for what you believe in my family." She sighed, and then she said, "I found out today I didn't get accepted into Cornish Hall. They said they were sure I was very talented and bright, but that I was too young to go away to school. They said it would be too difficult for me socially, and I should wait a year or two and apply again. Mom couldn't believe it. She said I could *learn* to be social. What was boarding school for if it wasn't for learning how to be social?"

"What about the other schools?"

"I did get into one of them, but it doesn't have a good music department, and it's in the middle of nowhere. I don't think it will be very easy to find a piano teacher if I end up going there. Cornish Hall was the only school I wanted to go to even one shred."

I stayed very still. Maybe sitting in the magical moonlit boathouse was helping Ivy talk more than usual. Or maybe it was helping me listen better and not get freaked out by serious things. "Ivy, what made you ask that question about the atom bomb?"

"I woke up in the middle of the night last night. The moon was shining into the Tower Room with this glowing white light, and the words *Hiroshima* and *Nagasaki* floated into my mind. We learned about the dropping of the bombs in history class this year. I remember sitting in the class, with the history textbook on my desk, and reading this one sentence: 'President Truman thought it was necessary to drop the bombs to end the war.'"

She paused for a moment, frowning the way she did when she was thinking about something.

"I had a Japanese piano teacher at camp," she went on. "And now that I know a little about Kiyoshi, it comes home to me that atomic bombs were dropped on a country where real people were living." She paused again, looking miserable. "I saw a film about the dropping of the bombs. It was so horrible. There was this flash of blinding white light, and people's shadows were frozen, and then there was all this radiation." She waved her hand in the air. "It makes me think about how atoms are in everything. They bond together to make a leaf or a bird or a finger, but when a single atom is torn apart, it tears everything apart." She sighed really deeply, and then she said, "I can't wait to see your parents. They're so nice, Holly, and they'll make everything seem better."

We were both quiet then, listening to the lapping water. And that was when we heard footsteps, and then suddenly Randy was standing in the doorway of the boathouse.

"Pointless!" Randy was muttering angrily to himself. "It's all so stupid." He strode over to the *Ginny* G and before we could call out to him, he began untying the boat, pulling her backward out of the stall. He jumped in and sat behind the wheel as the *Ginny* G coasted out of the boathouse. Ivy and I sat there like dummies, not saying anything. His back was to us, and he hadn't noticed us at all.

We drifted out into the moonlight. A slight breeze was blowing, and Randy shook his long hair off his face and turned the key, which was in the ignition. As the boat came to life, water spat out of the exhaust pipe and the air filled with fumes. We puttered slowly away from the dock, and then with one swift movement, Randy pushed the gear stick forward, and Ivy and I yelped as the bow lifted and the stern plunged down.

At first it was exciting to be out on the lake at night. We were racing up a path made of moonlight. But Randy suddenly spun the wheel hard over, and I was flung against the opposite side, and Ivy came crashing into me. Randy spun the wheel sharply in the other direction, and once again Ivy and I fell helplessly against each other. Randy whooped as we slapped down over our own wake. "Ride 'em, cowboy!" he yelled, standing at the wheel.

"We have to stop him," Ivy gasped.

We began making our way across the hatch of the engine, pressing our bodies flat against the wooden doors. As Randy spun the wheel again, I just managed to grab on to one of the handles, but Ivy's head snapped back with a *thwack*, and then she slid backward off the boat.

"Randy!" I screamed. "Randy, stop!"

Randy was in his own world. He didn't hear me. I dove for the bow, clearing the hatch, and landed head-first in the middle seat. Scrambling up, I looked frantically out on the lake for Ivy. Moonlight danced and shimmered everywhere, and then several yards away, I saw her arms splashing slightly as she treaded water.

"Ivy!" I screamed.

This time Randy turned to look at me, startled. The wheel turned with him, and the boat bucked as it changed course. A sheet of spray caught me in the face. The engine roared, and then we were speeding full-tilt toward the head in the water.

"Randy!" I screamed again. I threw myself over the back of his seat, trying desperately to get a grip on the steering wheel. Randy was too big for me to get past him. I reached for the key and yanked it out and threw it in the lake.

Holly
20

"Ivy, Ivy! Are you all right?" I was screaming again, and my voice echoed as it bounced off the shore. After the roar of the engine, everything seemed too quiet. I grabbed a paddle and scrambled onto the bow.

"I'm over here." Ivy's voice traveled faintly across the water.

"Hang on, Ivy, I'm trying to get over to you!" I sat as far forward as I could, straddling the bow, digging the paddle frantically into the water. Where *was* she? I couldn't *see* her.

And then there was another sound, a sort of rhythmic creaking. I turned to see bright colors in the moonlight.

Uncle Jake was rowing *Rainbow*, his back black and solid in the moonlight.

"Ivy's in the water! Over there!" I shouted and pointed, because I could see her now, not too far away.

The rowboat continued moving forward and then stopped.

"Lift your arms." Uncle Jake's voice carried eerily across the water. He leaned over the side of *Rainbow* and hauled Ivy out of the water like a sack of potatoes. "Is the motorboat out of gas?" he called out. "There's an extra tank in the stern."

"No," I said. "I threw the key in the water."

There was silence for a moment, and then Uncle Jake called out again. "Toss me the bow painter." His gruffness was strangely comforting.

I knelt on the bow and coiled the line, and then tossed it to Uncle Jake. He wrapped the end several times around the stern thwart.

Now, forward and back, forward and back, Uncle Jake rowed again. For the first time, I turned around and looked back at Randy. He was sitting slumped behind the wheel, his head in his hands.

The motorboat was so much heavier than the rowboat. We made slow, jerky progress. When we finally reached the dock, Grandpa and Gigi were there with Aunt Sandy and Sam—and then, their arms reaching out to me and pulling me close, so were Mom and Dad. I was crying now, my whole body shaking, but they felt solid and warm and safe, and Dad kept saying, "It's okay, Holly, it's okay."

Aunt Sandy helped Ivy out of the rowboat and wrapped her arms around her. "Run up to the house and get her a blanket," Aunt Sandy ordered Sam.

In the meantime, Aunt Sandy folded Ivy into a large beach towel as Randy brought the *Ginny G* into her stall. A moment later he stumbled out of the boathouse. He looked terrible. "It should have been me who got knocked out of the boat, not Ivy," he said, and his voice cracked. "The boat should have turned on me, and then you all wouldn't have to worry about what I do anymore—whether I go to school or war." He looked Uncle Jake squarely in the face. "It would be just like what happened to your brother all over again."

A terrible shudder ran through Uncle Jake. I was scared, and I pressed against Mom and Dad. Dad put his arms around me.

"I would never want what happened to my brother to happen to you," said Uncle Jake. He was staring down at the dock, speaking almost in a whisper.

"We really don't know what happened to him. We'll never know, because you'll never tell us," said Randy. He had begun to shout.

Mom left my side and went over to Uncle Jake. "You need to tell him, Jake," she said. "You almost lost your daughter tonight. And in a different way you're in danger of losing your son. Tell him now before it's too late."

"Please," said Grandpa. He looked old and frail and small. "What is all this?"

Sam came running down the hill with a blanket. As Aunt Sandy wrapped Ivy up in it, Mom said, "Go on, Jake. Tell him."

Uncle Jake moved so that he was standing almost directly in front of Randy. "It was the summer of 1941," he said. He spoke flatly, without any expression. Everyone else stayed still, clustered around him. "All of us Greenwood kids were off doing things that summer except for Jesse. I was working for an engineer, but Jesse was home, taking summer school classes at Hanford. But there were rumors of war, so I took a week off from my job and came home. I wanted to spend time with Jess before we both went off to college, or war, depending on what happened. But I came home to find a Japanese boy staying with the family—a student—one of Pa's students at Hanford."

"That boy," said Grandpa, choking slightly.

Mom reached out and put a hand on his arm. "Shhh, Pa, let him speak."

"That boy," Uncle Jake echoed. "His name was Kiyoshi. He and Jesse had become fast friends, and they were doing everything together. Going out in boats, fishing and hiking—all the kinds of things Jesse and I used to do together. They were always talking, too, talking about life in Japan, talking about the difference between our two cultures, how life was for the Japanese farmers in California—oh, you name it, they were talking about it. And I never seemed to be able to get Jesse to myself."

Now Uncle Jake began speaking in less of a monotone, and he lowered his head and clenched his fists. "On the last day of my week off, Jess took me aside. He said he needed to talk to me. He suggested we go out in the Ginny G because he wanted to be out of earshot of our parents. Of course, Kiyo had to come along. I drove, and Jesse sat beside me, but Kiyo sat right behind him, as if giving him moral support."

"You were driving the boat?" Grandpa seemed confused.

Uncle Jake groaned and rubbed a hand across his face. "Yes, I was driving the boat, but just let me tell you what happened. And then Jesse told me he wasn't going to go to Hanford as planned. He'd gotten it into his head he wanted to go to Berkeley, out in California. History repeats itself," he added flatly, glancing at Randy.

Grandpa looked grim. "If Kiyo wasn't driving—"

Mom put a hand on Grandpa's arm. "Let him talk now, Pa."

"I was driving the boat, and Jesse was beside me, and Kiyo was sitting behind us," Uncle Jake repeated heavily. "Jesse was perched up on the seat, sitting on his heels, talking a mile a minute. He was spouting what I'm sure he thought were all these lofty ideas—that if we did go to war, he wasn't going to fight because he didn't believe in killing people. He said he was going to college in California so he could help the Japanese workers out there. And there was that boy sitting behind him, nodding at everything Jesse was saying. And I became so angry, I could hardly see straight. My own brother, I realized, was a coward, and not only that, he was not a patriot. I flung out my arm, and I pushed him, and because he was perched up there, not sitting flat on the seat, he lost his balance, and he went flying. His head hit the side of the boat, and then he fell out. I let go of the steering wheel, and the boat—"

I closed my eyes, and Dad's arms tightened around me. *That's enough,* I thought. *We all know what happened next.*

But Uncle Jake didn't stop. "I came to my senses and yanked the wheel over, and at the same time, I cut the engine. But I hadn't acted quickly enough." He held up both his hands now, close to his face. They were shaking badly.

"It's all right, Jake, don't—" Gigi tried to say, but Uncle Jake broke in.

"I threw myself into the lake, and when I reached Jess, he was floating facedown in a cloud of blood. I turned him over. I didn't know if he was alive or dead, but I got him in a grip, swam him back to shore, and after a moment, he came to. But his leg was gashed open. He was bleeding—so much blood. I found a towel—tied it tight." He shook his head. "I'm telling you, that moment was worse than anything I ever lived through in the damn war. I almost killed my own brother."

Sam clutched his father's arm. "You didn't kill him, Dad. You *saved* his life." Uncle Jake stared at Sam. "You *saved* his life, Dad," Sam repeated, more loudly this time.

In the moonlight, I could see sweat pouring down Uncle Jake's face. "The irony is, because of me, Jesse's leg was mangled," he said hoarsely. "No earthly use to the army, that's for sure, even if he had wanted to be a soldier. And in the end, he went to work in a Jap camp."

"So Uncle Jesse went to work in a relocation camp," said Randy.

"Yes, and that's where he died," said Uncle Jake. "Shot in an uprising. Inmates rioting. Just like that. A shameful death."

No one said a word. Everyone stood as still as statues, casting shadows in the moonlight.

"But Kiyo—when we came down to the dock that day, Kiyo was at the helm of the motorboat," Grandpa said.

Uncle Jake turned to him. "Don't you understand what I'm trying to tell you? When Jesse was injured, I was driving the boat."

"But—" Grandpa kept shaking his head. "We thought—"

"I know what you thought. And I let you believe it. And so did Kiyo, for reasons I'll never understand. But I'm telling you, he wasn't driving the boat."

Grandpa raised his trembling hands into the air. "You mean to tell me you let that boy take the blame for what happened to Jesse?"

Uncle Jake stood motionless.

Grandpa stared down at his feet, half mumbling as if he were talking to himself. "I said unforgivable things. I swore at him, shouted at him. I told that poor young boy he should have stayed in his own country, and what was he doing here, anyway?" He paused, and then turned to look at Gigi. "I will admit, when I was calmer, I questioned the whole thing. He had always seemed so gentle. It was hard for me to imagine him tearing about in the motorboat." He grunted slightly. "I remember thinking the three of you must have been drinking."

It was quiet on the dock again. My legs felt rubbery. I leaned into Dad, wishing we could sit down.

"I saw Kiyo on campus after that, of course," Grandpa went on, "and I thought about approaching him any number of times. After all, it was clearly an accident. He hadn't meant it to happen. But then when Jesse died—I never did speak to him again. If I saw him on campus, I walked the other way." Grandpa raised a trembling finger in the air and pointed it at Uncle Jake. "And you let him take the blame..." His voice trailed off.

Uncle Jake nodded. "I am the true coward, the son who never had the courage to tell the truth. I let Kiyoshi take the blame because—because he was foreign, soon to become our enemy. The way I saw it back then, I figured it didn't matter."

Sam pulled slightly on Uncle Jake's arm. "There *was* a war going on, Dad," he said. "It's the kind of thing people do in wars."

Uncle Jake shook his head. "No," he said. "No, it isn't."

"I never for a moment believed it was Kiyo driving the boat," said Gigi quietly. "But I never believed, either, Jake, that you meant to harm your brother."

Uncle Jake crumpled. Right there on the dock, he fell to his knees. The look on his face was terrible, and then Ivy lurched out of Aunt Sandy's arms. She staggered over to the edge of the dock, and then she was sick, and everyone rushed to help her.

Holly
21

I tossed and turned all night. I dreamed Ivy was falling into the lake, or was it Uncle Jake? No, it wasn't Uncle Jake—it was me, under the water, with the churning of the propeller in my ears.

I startled awake. It took me a minute to realize where I was because I wasn't used to the room. I was sleeping in my parents' bedroom and in my parents' bed. The room was darker than the Tower Room, and I could just make out the lumpy forms of Mom and Dad under the blankets. Mom woke up and put her arms around me. "Go back to sleep, Holly," she said, but now I was worried about Ivy. They had taken her to the hospital. They said she had thrown up because she had a concussion, and she had to be watched carefully.

Ivy came home from the hospital, but she had to stay quiet for a few days. She wasn't allowed to be out in the sun or running around. Gigi set her up on the couch in the living room, and we took turns reading aloud to her.

When the aunts and uncles weren't around, Tina said, "So Uncle Jesse didn't die being run over by the motorboat."

"I swear I heard Uncle John and Uncle Jimmy saying he was," said Sam.

Randy said, "You heard wrong."

Dad took me mushroom hunting. He showed me the morels, which are the best mushrooms for eating.

And then Mom said she wanted to spend some time with me alone. "How about we row *Rainbow* out to Secret Cove?" she said.

When we got there we climbed up on the bank and sat on the log Uncle Jake and I had sat on. "Anytime one of us needed a place to go to that was away from the others, we'd come here," Mom said. "It's where I found Jake after we learned of Jesse's death. I think before Jesse died, Jake barely even noticed he had a little sister—but there I was, in the right place at the right time, and he poured his heart out to me. He told me how jealous he was of Kiyoshi Mori. And then he told me he wished he had been on better terms with Jesse before he died. But he never told me what really happened in the boat. Like the rest of the family, I believed Kiyo had been the one driving the motorboat when Jesse was injured. It's curious that I never questioned the story, but on the other hand, I never actually met Kiyo. I like to think that if I had, I wouldn't have believed it.

"But I always had the impression that over the years something was slowly poisoning Jake, destroying his peace of mind. I wish you'd known Jake when he was young, Holly. He was as good-natured as they come."

She smiled ruefully and then reached out and stroked my hair. "You have a slightly new look. It's nice."

"Tina Greenwood's Beauty Salon," I said. "But go on, Mom. I want to know what research you were doing out in California."

"I'm getting to that," she said. "Jake was so awful at Thanksgiving, barking at Sam, criticizing Ivy, being downright mean to Sandy. Terrible uproar with Randy at the table. So I screwed up my courage and wrote him a long letter saying I was worried about him. It took him a while, but he finally wrote me back asking if we could meet somewhere. So we did, and he told me what really had happened on that boat. It seems that allowing Kiyo to take the blame for injuring Jesse is what has been eating at him all these years."

"That's terrible," I said. "Poor Uncle Jake."

Mom nodded. "He told me he wrote Kiyo dozens of letters but never had the courage to send them. And then when he finally contacted the college to see if he could get his address, he learned that Kiyo had died of cancer. Jake thought now he could never make things right. But he did learn that Kiyo's widow was living in San Francisco. So, Holly, *that's* why I jumped at the opportunity to go out there with Dad. I thought if I could find her, I could at least explain things to her."

"Did you find her?"

Mom shook her head. "I found relatives Kiyo and his wife had stayed with, but Mrs. Mori had already returned to Japan. You see, when Kiyo learned he was ill and didn't have long to live, he went only briefly to San Francisco to see a young man who had grown up in one of the relocation camps. Kiyo had sponsored this young man for many years and wanted to see him one more time before he died. Sadly, Kiyo passed away after only a few weeks of being there."

"Uncle Jake could write to her and explain things," I said. "That would be better than nothing."

"Yes, he could," said Mom, nodding. "And I hope he will. You can imagine, though, Holly, how startled I was to get your letter asking about Uncle Jesse. Almost as if you could sense what I was doing out there."

We were quiet for a while then. I picked at the bark of the log, thinking. "Mom," I said finally, "if I tell you something, promise you won't laugh at me? I think Jesse and Kiyo wanted us to find out about them."

"What do you mean?" Mom asked. She'd been gazing out at the lake, but now she turned to look at me.

"I've sort of *felt* them off and on, as if they'd been trying to get me to pay attention to them. Things kept turning up—a painting, photographs, Uncle Jesse's diary, letters—"

Mom looked thoughtful. "Maybe it was time for them to be remembered," she said. "Secrets aren't good for people. So Jesse and Kiyo kept pushing to come out of the dark, secret corner they'd been stuffed into—and you're not a secretive kind of person, Holly. You were just the person to bring them into the light."

She stood up and walked down the bank and picked a bunch of forget-me-nots. "Jesse was such a—I don't know, he was like sunlight on the lake—he lifted your spirits. He was fun, but he could be serious, too. And Kiyo. I know I would have liked him if I'd known him. So let's not forget either of them. Let's make a memorial to both of them out here."

She knelt and placed the flowers by a tree, and I walked down and joined her.

The entire family was going into Glover for Miranda's performance. We headed in early because people had all sorts of things to do in town—Peter wanted to go to the bookstore, Gigi wanted to check on the garden at the winter house. Aunt Kate took Tina and Tucker and the twins shopping for clothes. Aunt Sandy took Ivy, and I got to go shopping with my own mother and father. I bought a blue dress that I adored.

Grandpa had made arrangements for Ivy to play on a good piano at the college, so after shopping, Ivy and I headed across Hanford Common to the music department.

"This is so neat," Ivy said as we walked down a hall. "All these practice rooms. And look," she said, stopping suddenly. She pointed to a poster of a black-haired man in a tuxedo seated at a piano. "That's Tōru Kameda. He's the man who came and taught the master classes at my camp. I can't believe it! He's giving a concert right here in Glover. I sure would like to go to that."

I sat in a corner of the practice room with my sketchbook while Ivy played. Her head was tilted toward the keys, her face deep in concentration. She wasn't just Ivy when she was playing—she was part of the music. I could almost see the notes pouring out of her brain, running down her arm and into her fingers. I thought of how Tina had said so scornfully, "She's just so *special*."

Watching Ivy and listening to her, I thought: She *is* special.

When Ivy finally stopped playing, she stretched her arms and flexed her fingers and said, "Wow! What a difference a good piano makes. The keys don't stick, and it's actually been tuned."

"Your playing always sound perfect to me," I said.

"That's because you don't know anything," Ivy said. Then she grinned. "Sorry! That sounded terrible."

I sighed, thinking that actually, when she wasn't playing the piano, Ivy wasn't special. She was annoying.

And then we went over to Gigi and Grandpa's house, where we changed into our good clothes, and then we met everyone for supper at a restaurant before going to the play.

Supper was fun—the Greenwood family took up half the restaurant. All the grown-ups looked spiffy in their summer jackets or summer dresses, and all the kids looked shiny as well. The twins were cute in matching dresses, with bows in their hair. Tucker had gotten a haircut, which made him look older. Tina's hair had honey highlights from the sun and was pulled back with a pink hairband. Her cheeks were tanned and rosy, and she looked great in a new pink dress. Ivy was wearing a white collared blouse and a navy-blue skirt and knee socks. That was dressed up for her. Sam was in Uncle Jesse's old jacket. It occurred to me, too, how much happier he seemed lately. His face seemed fuller and less baby-birdish. Randy and Peter were handsome in completely different ways. Peter, in a tweed jacket, already looked like a college professor, and Randy, in a white shirt and vest with his hair tied back, looked like—I don't know—Paul Revere.

And I was wearing my new and beautiful blue dress.

After supper, we milled around outside the theater waiting to go in. Ned was standing with his parents, looking uncomfortable in a corduroy jacket and a nice pair of pants. He came over and pretty soon took off his jacket and slung it over his arm, and he and I hung out by the hydrangeas and petunias. He kept saying things that made me laugh, and the air was warm and smelled of perfume and tobacco and flowers. The sky was striped storm gray and sunset red. And somehow all the scents and colors got mixed in with how much I liked Ned.

Tina came up to him and asked, "Is Will coming?"

Ned shrugged and said, "I'm not sure."

And then it was time to go in. As we settled into our long row made up of family members, I saw that Ned was sitting with his parents two rows behind us. I opened the program. There in print it said: Miranda Greenwood...Luciana.

Ivy sat on one side of me reading the program, and Tina was on the other side. She kept craning her neck around, and I guessed she was looking for Will. She suddenly gasped and immediately looked straight down at her program. I turned, and there was Will, dressed in a snappy jacket, sitting down next to Ned. A dark-haired girl sat down with him. I watched as he draped his arm across the back of her chair, and then their heads were nearly touching as they studied the program. Will looked up, saw me, smiled, and waved. Tina sat frozen, staring rigidly down at her program.

The house lights dimmed, and the audience cleared throats, rustled programs, coughed. And the curtains opened.

Miranda had told us the play was about a pair of twins and their servants, who are also twins and are separated at birth and then end up in the same city without realizing it. People keep running into one or the other of the twins, mistaking them for their husband or the person who owes them money. Even though the title, A Comedy of Errors, tells you it's a comedy, I didn't expect it to be as hilarious as it was. I thought Miranda was especially funny. She was playing the sister of the wife of one of the twins. Everyone was laughing and laughing, except for Tina, who was still staring straight down at her lap. She wasn't even watching the play.

A clap of thunder punctuated the end of the first act. The lights came up for intermission. The doors at the back of the theater opened, but it was pouring outside. Ivy and Tucker and Ned and I headed for the covered porch, where refreshments were being served.

"Look," said Ivy, grabbing my arm. "Over there. It's Tōru Kameda."

"Go and say something to him," I said.

Ivy looked horrified. "No, I couldn't do that."

"Of course you can. Tell him you met him at camp—he'll probably remember you."

"I can't," said Ivy. She began twisting her program in agony. "And I *doubt* he'll remember me."

"I'll go with you." I started to drag Ivy by the arm, but Tina came flying over to us. "Hide me," she said. "You have to hide me."

But Will and the dark-haired girl were already approaching, walking hand in hand. "Hey, Greenwoods, I want you all to meet my friend, Emily. Emily, these are the kids I told you I've been teaching—Holly and Ivy, and Tina—and my *gosh*, Miranda is talented."

"Remind me never to speak to that flirt-bag again," said Tina in a low voice as Will and Emily walked away.

Act two. Miranda's line came up, the one she had been having trouble with. The row of Greenwoods tensed up to say the line with her. And then the play got really ridiculous as things became more and more tangled, but then everything got sorted out in the end. I was so proud of Miranda as the cast came out for a bow, and everyone clapped really hard for her.

As one by one the actors emerged from the dressing room, Miranda was surrounded by admiring fans. The family hung back slightly so that other people could get to her. Tōru Kameda was one of her fans.

"You were magnificent," he said, stepping forward and shaking her hand. "Such a flair for comedy!"

"Thank you," Miranda said. Her cheeks were flushed and her eyes were dancing with excitement.

"I see that your last name is Greenwood," he said. "You aren't, by chance, any relation of the Greenwood family that lives here in Glover— there is a Professor Greenwood—"

Miranda looked at the musician curiously now, and all of us Greenwoods shifted as one group toward him. He was a short, slight man, with a high forehead and an intense expression on his face. His hair was long, and his eyes were very bright.

"I am Professor Greenwood," said Grandpa. "That is, I'm Ted Greenwood, retired professor."

Tōru Kameda's face lit up. He strode toward Grandpa and grabbed his hand and shook it and then held on to it as if he would never let it go. "Yes, yes!" he exclaimed. "Please—I have so much to say to you—to all of you. But not here, not now. I have a very busy schedule for the next few days, but I would like to find a time to come see you."

His accent was very American. "And I have a letter to give you—Mrs. Greenwood—" He turned to look at all of us again, searching for Gigi. She moved slightly toward him. "From Kiyoshi Mori," he said.

"From Kiyo!" she cried out.

"I will come to your house in a few days and tell you everything, all right?"

Holly
22

Ivy couldn't stop pacing around. "When Tōru Kameda comes here, should I ask him to listen to me play something?" she asked.

"Of course," I said.

"But it will seem so forward of me—conceited."

"No, it'll be natural. You just have to tell him you're playing for the competition—or no, I'll mention it to him, you don't even have to—and then he'll say, 'Oh, what are you playing for it?' and you'll tell him, and he'll say, 'Why don't you play it for me?' And you will, and then he'll offer to help you while we're still here at Otter Lake."

Ivy's eyes sparkled. "Do you think so? Do you think he'll say that?"

"Of course!"

"Tōru Kameda is coming *here*," said Ivy, hugging herself.

We spent every waking moment working on the Greenwood play. Now that her own play was over, Miranda was rehearsing us all the time.

Tigs and Tally were playing the guards, and they had us rolling on the floor. They were both so serious, snapping out their commands, which made them unbearably funny. Sam was a great villain, and Peter was wonderful both as the dying king at the beginning of the play and as the bishop at the end. His English accent was perfect for both parts. Tucker was a perfect hero, too.

But...Tina was truly terrible. Everything she said was flat and expressionless.

"Tina," Miranda said in desperation, "can't you talk the way you do in real life? Why do you make every line you speak sound as if you're reciting a grocery list?"

"Is Will Brown invited to this play?" Tina asked. "Because if he is, I'm not doing it."

Miranda marched off and came back half an hour later saying, "Will Brown is not coming. He is otherwise engaged."

And Tina got slightly better.

The day before the play was being performed, Ivy and I were sitting out on the porch playing cards after supper.

"Don't you think it's strange?" she said. "All the twin things this summer? *The Prince and the Pauper, The Comedy of Errors,* and Dad and Uncle Jesse?"

She said the name, Uncle Jesse, just like that. No hesitating or lowering her voice or looking awkward.

Miranda appeared and asked, "Do you know what you're going to play for your musical interlude, Ivy? I'm sorry I haven't really had a chance to talk to you about it."

"I don't know," said Ivy. "I'll think of something."

"I was just curious because Tōru Kameda and his family are coming for their visit tomorrow, and they're staying for the play."

"What?" Ivy leaped up, scattering cards everywhere.

"Gigi invited them."

"Ivy knows exactly what she's going to play," I said. "Don't you?"

"I guess," she said.

I got up and grabbed her by the arm. "Come on, Ivy, we're going down to the Sunbird."

Down at the tree, we stood face to face and put out our hands and placed them on the Sunbird. My wish: *Please let Ivy play really well for Tōru Kameda and not be too nervous.*

I don't know what Ivy's wish was, but I was pretty sure it was a lot like mine.

Tōru Kameda and his family arrived just before lunch. Gigi and the aunts had spent hours fluttering around, worrying about what we should eat. "What if they don't like American food?" Aunt Kate kept asking.

"Tōru was born in the United States," Randy said.

"How do you know that?" Aunt Kate asked.

"There are brochures about him everywhere in Glover with a little bio," said Randy, "and every one of them says he spent most of his life in California. So I think he'll manage to eat a chicken salad sandwich."

Any shyness or nervousness we might have felt melted the moment the Kamedas arrived. Both Tōru and his wife, Midori, were friendly and warm and easy, and their little boy, Kiyo, instantly became attached to Tigs and Tally. Randy was right—chicken salad sandwiches seemed to be just fine. We ate outside on the terrace in the dappled shade of the giant pines. It was a perfect day, a "real New Hampshire day," as Grandpa liked to say. The sun was shining, the sky was blue, and Gigi had set pots of red geraniums all around.

After ice cream (made by Grandpa) and cookies (made by Tigs and Tally), Tōru said, "I want to tell you a story now."

Uncle Jake, I realized, was nowhere to be seen, but the rest of us pulled our chairs into a circle. Midori sat beside Tōru while Kiyo played on the terrace near her feet. And Tōru began to speak.

He told us how his father's parents had been farmers back in Japan, but it was not an easy life, and his father, at the age of eighteen, decided to leave Japan and go to America, hoping to find new opportunities. He lived in Hawaii for a while but soon found work as a houseboy for a wealthy American on the mainland. He became the all-around handyman, chauffeur, and cook. And then he met a woman who was selling vegetables at the market, and he fell in love with her almost the moment he saw her. They soon got married. Her father was a hardworking farmer in the area, and Tōru's dad left the wealthy American's home and went to work on his new wife's family's farm.

Tōru's voice was pleasant, and he was very easy to listen to. "You younger folk might not realize what it was like for Japanese people back in those days. There was something called the Alien Land Laws. The Issei—that is, the first-generation Japanese—were prevented from owning property. But my grandparents leased the land they were farming, and through very hard work, they were able to make a decent living. So much so that by the time my sister and I were born, we were able to have a nice life. We were surrounded by peach and plum and apple trees. One of my favorite memories is all the fragrant blossoms in spring. And the harvests in the fall—there was so much bounty!" He smiled for a moment, but then he leaned forward in his chair, looking more serious. "And then came the bombing of Pearl Harbor, and families like ours were swept up and carried off to camps.

"I know for you younger folk, too, it is hard to imagine the atmosphere of fear and suspicion of those times. Every person of Japanese descent was suspected of sending secret signals to all the Japanese submarines they imagined were lurking along the coast." Tōru shook his head. "I understand this point of view a little better now," he said. "Bombs had been dropped." He paused again, looking up for a moment, as if scanning the sky for warplanes. Midori put a hand on his arm, and he looked down and began to speak again. "Over two thousand people were killed on December seventh, the day of Pearl Harbor. About seventy of them were innocent civilians—not people in the armed forces at all. They were just people—like you, like me." He frowned and shook his head again. "But when we start counting like that, what good does it do? This many Americans died as prisoners of war in the Philippines, and this many Japanese died as prisoners of war in Russia." He began ticking off groups of people on his fingers. "And this many Jews were killed in German camps, and this many Chinese were killed by Japanese bombs, and don't forget all the Japanese who died at Hiroshima and Nagasaki." He held up a finger. "And we haven't finished counting that last one, because people are still falling ill from the radiation."

Midori glanced at Kiyo, who was building a little house out of twigs. Tōru followed her glance. "But this is not good conversation for children to hear," he said more quietly. "What I came here to tell you today, and what I want you to know is, when my family and I were in the camp, there was a young man there who was my teacher. His name was Jesse Greenwood."

Tōru was looking directly at Grandpa now.

"I was ten years old at the time," he said, "and every day I looked forward to being taught by this tall, friendly Caucasian who walked with a limp. We, the children of Japanese descent, had all been yanked out of our schools, you see, and there wasn't any formal schooling set up at the camp yet. This young man read out loud to us. He set us math problems and encouraged us to write stories. And as long as he was teaching us, he made us forget we were in this dreary camp where it was often so cold, where we were often so hungry.

"And then, many months went by. There was more and more unhappiness at the camp and a lot of tension—not only between the inmates and the supervisors, but between different factions among the Japanese themselves. There were many angry people among us who did not trust the Caucasians. They said we should go back to Japan and leave behind the United States, this country that had mistreated us so. There were others who said no—this, too, shall pass, and things will get better.

"One day, a man who had spoken up against the authorities was arrested. He had been very popular, and there was a huge march of protest against his arrest. I remember being very frightened, of holding tight to Jesse Greenwood's hand because the protest erupted during school hours. I remember the wave of people surging forward, and shouting angrily, and then the police threw tear gas. Some of our people pushed a truck at the jail where the man was being held prisoner. The police started shooting into the crowd—and that is when Jesse Greenwood stepped in front of me—to protect me—and there was a bullet—" Tōru broke off, swallowing hard. He seemed unable to go on.

Grandpa groaned, and Gigi, who was sitting next to him, found his hand and held it.

Holly

23

"We knew he died in the camp," said Gigi softly. "We knew there had been a protest of some kind, but we never knew the exact circumstances."

"Jesse was taken to the camp hospital," Tōru said slowly and quietly. "He held on for five days." He didn't say anything for a long moment, as if allowing us to take this in. "I am so sorry," he said finally. "But now you know that your son was a hero, as brave as any soldier who fought in a war."

Randy was near me, sitting up very straight and tall. Aunt Sandy and Ivy and Sam were all sitting close together, leaning into each other.

Tōru took a breath. "Soon after that," he said "there came another challenge. Everyone who was seventeen or older was required to fill out a loyalty oath. Were you willing to serve in the armed forces of the United States, it asked, and would you also swear unqualified allegiance to the US and faithfully defend it from attack?"

"Even though you were denied your freedoms by the government, they wanted you to fight for it," Randy put in angrily.

Tōru nodded. "It was very difficult. Making the decision to say yes or no to the questions tore apart many families. If you refused to sign, you'd very likely be sent back to Japan. People like my father didn't want to return there. As bad as things were for him in the US, Papa didn't want to start over. He understood, too, that the most effective way a Japanese man could prove his loyalty to the US was to go and fight. And so Papa did just that. He joined up and served in the army. It turned out to be a very hard time for my family. We missed him terribly. On top of that, for me, also, was the trauma of having been standing with Jesse when he was shot. I had nightmares. Every night I would wake up crying."

A chipmunk ran by. Kiyo squealed with delight, pointing to it. Tōru leaned down and pulled the little boy into his lap.

"Things at the camp gradually improved," Tōru continued. "Life slowly became more normal. A real school was opened. All kinds of gardens were planted. There was now enough food. There were barber-shops and Boy Scouts. There were softball leagues and glee clubs. Ironi-cally, it was in the camp that I first realized how much I loved music. There were so many people thrown together there, from all walks of life. My first piano teacher was an old Issei who didn't have a single tooth in his head, but what a musician he was! The restraints on us gradually loos-ened up: people were even allowed to go 'outside' and find jobs inland. And then, in 1944, the Supreme Court ruled that loyal citizens could not be held against their will in detention camps. That strange, terrible time was finally over. But curiously, after Papa came home, he immediately sent me back to Japan. After everything, he wanted me to go live for a while with my Japanese grandparents, to learn some of the old traditional ways."

Kiyo was drawing circles with a twig on Tōru's shirt.

"During those years, I often thought about Jesse Greenwood. I thought about his family. I wanted to meet them and say thank you—to repay them in some way for his sacrifice. But I was so far away from every-thing, living on my grandparents' farm. I didn't know how to find the Greenwood family. Meanwhile, Kiyoshi Mori, who had gone to college in the United States, returned to Japan. Through relatives who had been in California at the time, he learned of Jesse Greenwood's story, how he had died saving a Japanese boy's life. He wanted to find that boy, and as he was from a wealthy and powerful family, he had long arms and many resources. When I was thirteen, to my great surprise, Kiyo found me on my grandparents' farm.

"From that moment on, Kiyoshi Mori took me under his wing. He paid for me to go to good schools. He nourished my musical talent. He provided me with the best teachers, the best training. As a result of his kindness, I have lived for many years studying and teaching in San Fran-cisco. And the very last thing he did for me before he died was to secure a teaching appointment at Hanford College. He saw my being here as a means of completing a circle. Hanford, he said, was where the Japanese connection to New Hampshire had all begun. And now, Mrs. Green-wood, I have two letters for you—"

"Please call me Gigi," said Gigi. "It's so much easier, and everyone does."

"Well then, Gigi," said Tōru with a smile. He gently handed Kiyo to

Midori, and then he opened a leather satchel he had resting at his feet. He pulled out two envelopes. "This first one I have carried with me since I was ten years old. Jesse wrote this in the hospital as he was dying." He handed the letter to Gigi. She opened it slowly and began reading. When she finished, she gave it to Grandpa.

"And this one is to you from Kiyoshi Mori," said Tōru, handing Gigi another envelope. "Please forgive me for not sending it sooner. I wanted to meet you and give it to you in person."

Gigi read the second letter, and soon gave that one to Grandpa to read, too.

Then Gigi said, "There will be no more secrets in this family. I will share these letters with my family."

And sitting there in her denim dress (her "dress-up" dress for Otter Lake), with her curly gray hair pulled back by a headband, Gigi read the first letter from Kiyo.

January, 1965

My dear Mrs. Greenwood-san,

Many years have gone by, and every single day that has passed, I have thought of you. It was very difficult for me after you told me it would be better not to write letters anymore because you were afraid it might be unfair to keep secrets from your husband. But not being able to write you has been very difficult for me. It is as if a part of my heart has been cut out.

All those years ago, in that one last letter you wrote to me, you said you saw me in the back of the chapel at Hanford, and all you wanted to do was put your arms around me and say what happened to Jesse was not my fault. I can barely write the words, Mrs. Greenwood, for the tears that are falling. I am so grateful that you were never full of hatred toward me. On that day of mourning for Jesse, I saw you surrounded by your family. Mrs. Greenwood, I was glad for you, to be surrounded by so many who loved you, but I wanted to speak to you, to reach out, but I knew I must not. I had heard all sorts of rumors—that Jesse had been killed in a Japanese camp.

I knew then there was no hope at all of Mr. Greenwood ever speaking to me again. There were many on campus who had tolerated me reasonably well up until then but who now shunned me. Some even threatened me with violence. It was not their fault. There was too much sorrow in the world then for people to make sense of anything.

The war has been over for many years now. I should have written to you, except that I have been afraid of opening up old wounds, upsetting Professor Greenwood again—although I have learned recently that it was he who went to President Clemens to promote my cause. In spite of everything he might have believed about me, he asked that I be allowed to stay at the college. I believe President Clemens respected Professor Greenwood more than any other instructor in the college, and in the end, I believe his support made the difference.

In any case, a change in my state of affairs has pressed upon me the need to reach out to you. My dear Mrs. Greenwood, the truth is, I am not well—I am sorry to say, not well at all, and I do not have a long time left to me. And so that is why I am writing to you now, for there are many things I must say.

In the first place, I must express gratitude: I have so many fond memories of staying with you and your family on the lake. I have warm memories of many of my classmates, too; they were good friends to me during a terrible time between our two countries. You, and they, were so generous to put up with having an enemy in your midst. How brave it was of your husband and the college to stand by me.

In the second place, I must talk about what happened in the motorboat so long ago. My dear Mrs. Greenwood, although you never came out and said so, I have always been comforted by the knowledge that you seemed to understand that I did not cause Jesse's injury. And all these years later, I ask myself, in my effort to protect Jake, did I not do him more harm than good?

And finally, I am writing this as a letter of introduction for Tōru Kameda. As perhaps you know, a cousin of mine became friends with Jesse when they were both living at the International House at the University of California at Berkeley. When war was declared, my cousin returned home immediately—already being on the West Coast, he had no trouble catching the first boat home—but he had friends who were interned at the camp where Jesse worked. We learned, as time went on, of Jesse's enormous bravery. This was not at all surprising to me, but in the end, his final act of heroism always leaves me speechless with tears.

I hope you will receive Tōru Kameda and his family with open hearts. Jesse's gift to us was preserving the life of this truly gifted musician.

Mrs. Greenwood-san, one more thing. In the last few years, I realized my dream: I have been running a camp for boys and girls out in the countryside of Japan. It has made me very happy! It is you who always said to me, if you have a dream, Kiyo, then you must follow it!

I hope so much that one day, my lovely wife and my dear sons will be able to meet you, too. And as you read this, don't be sad, Mrs. Greenwood. As our poet Matsuo Basho wrote so many centuries ago:

The temple bell dies away.
The scent of flowers in the evening
Is still tolling the bell.

With love and gratitude,
Kiyoshi Mori

Gigi wiped her eyes and then, collecting herself, turned to Grandpa. "I think, Ted, that I have also caused more harm than good, thinking I was protecting you. Jesse wrote me, you see, telling me he was going to go to work in the relocation camp—telling me he wasn't going to enlist or allow himself to be enlisted. I kept the letters from you, Ted, thinking you would not be able to bear knowing that your own son refused to be a soldier."

Grandpa shifted slightly, holding his trembling hands tightly together in his lap.

"I am so sorry, Ted," said Gigi. "If I hadn't kept these things from you, you could have gradually adjusted to the idea. The shock wouldn't have been so great."

Grandpa reached over and put a hand on Gigi's arm. "Hush, now. You were only doing what you thought was right. I am the one who behaved as if I'd break in two if his name was ever mentioned. The truth is, I knew all this about him without having to be told, and I didn't have the courage to stand up for him. I buried my own son without ever giving him the chance to express himself to me."

He took the second letter from Gigi, and then he read it out loud. It was the bravest thing I have ever seen anyone do.

Dear Mother and Dad,

I don't know if this letter will ever get to you, but I can only pray it does. I believe I only have a few hours left to me. Please know that I have not lived my life in vain. I have done everything I have ever wanted to do, and that is because I grew up in freedom, under the sun and the stars, in the wind, in the water, on the waves. My only regret is leaving my twin to live his life alone—he is half of me, my practical, smarter half, my bodyguard, my best friend, and wherever I am going next, I will always miss him. And finally, my dear parents, please stand at the tree where Kiyoshi Mori and I carved our own flag, combining the symbols of our two countries— the red sun and the eagle—and make a wish, that the people of this earth will learn to live in peace.

Your loving son,
Jesse

Ivy's diary
Thursday, August 27, 1965

A few days ago, when Tōru came here to Otter Lake House with his family, he told us how Uncle Jesse saved his life. And then that night, we put on the Greenwood end-of-summer play. It was a very funny play. Holly makes me laugh even more than Miranda. I don't know how she does it, but she has these funny expressions, and she's just so hilarious.

The way Miranda had written the play, there wasn't a fencing scene, but Holly suddenly picked up a flower (she was the flower girl), and she handed Tina one, too, and she started attacking Tina with her flower. Up until then, Tina had been saying everything in this monotone voice, but now she had to fight back, and she started screaming like good old Tina. It was the funniest thing I have ever seen. Ned and his parents came. Not Will, thank goodness. All the aunts and uncles were there, and Grandpa and Gigi, of course, and Randy, and Tōru and Midori and little Kiyo. Everyone laughed so hard, and Gigi was crying from laughing so hard. It was the best way a day so full of emotion could have ended.

But for me, it wasn't an ending at all—it was a beginning! Because in the intermission I played the piece Tōru had composed. When I finished playing, Tōru sprang out of his chair and said, "What a lovely surprise to hear you playing that!" Then he said he had been looking at me all day trying to figure out where he had seen me before. But the moment I started playing, he knew immediately who I was—I was the Mozart girl from the master class at the music camp.

And then, because he is very polite, he let the rest of the play go on.

When the play was over, everyone wanted to go for a swim. So everyone went down to the dock, but Tōru asked me to stay behind so he could talk to me. He asked me who my teacher was, and I told him right now I didn't have one. And then I told him my situation—how I don't know where I'm going to school next year, but that I am going out for a competition at the end of September, and I'm worried about it. Tōru has these eyes—he makes you feel as if he's really listening to you. He asked if I could come into Glover and play for him on a real piano, and of course I said yes.

So yesterday Randy drove me to Glover. I met Tōru in one of the practice rooms in the music department. At first I was nervous, but pretty soon the music took over. Maybe, too, I was feeling a kind of freedom. When Tōru was coming to visit, Gigi made us stand on the dining room table with a duster and reach up and swipe away all the cobwebs. I think all the anger and tension that sometimes swirled around us during meals were caught in those cobwebs, and now they've all been swept away.

And so I played. And then Tōru asked me to play other pieces. And then when I had finished, he asked me how old I was. I said thirteen. He said musically I was going on thirty, but inside, maybe I was only ten. Because of that, he said I should wait a year before entering the competition. He told me I must not rush things. And in the meantime, I should study with a good teacher.

I said, "Yes, I should. I can live with my grandparents here in Glover and go to school here and study with you."

Tōru put back his head and roared with laughter, and he said, "What a good idea!"

So then I talked to Mom and Dad. For a *long* time. And Tōru talked to Gigi and Grandpa. For a *long* time. And then everybody talked to everybody else. *Forever.* But *finally* it's all arranged. I'm going to live with Grandpa and Gigi and go to the public school in Glover. Gigi said it was a good enough school for all the Greenwood children, and it's good enough for the grandchildren.

I am so full of happiness that if you poured one more drop into me, I wouldn't be able to take it in. The last few days have been so—I don't even have the words for any of it. One thing: Gigi gave Dad Uncle Jesse's letter to read. He went off by himself to read it, and then he came back. No one has dared ask him about it. It's like one of those old sayings—a leopard can't change its spots. I mean, our family can't instantly turn into a family that talks openly about things.

But Mom and Dad were walking on the beach yesterday, and they were holding hands. I'm beginning to feel as if I can breathe a little easier.

And now I must write these two words: Tōru Kameda.

I want to learn how to write the Japanese characters for his name.

A little later... Holly said there was something she wanted to show me and to come with her down to the Sunbird Tree. So we went down the hill and we stopped there. I reached out to trace the carving with my fingers, thinking about Jesse and Kiyo coming up with the idea of the Sunbird all those years ago.

Then Holly walked around to the other side of the tree. She had a funny smile on her face as she stood there and pointed. And there was a carving of a funny-looking animal. It had the head of a rabbit and the body of a deer.

"That's a bundeer," she said.

"A what?" I said.

She grinned. "A bundeer. I'm the bunny rabbit, and you're the deer."

"A bundeer," I said, and started to giggle. Then I reached out and touched the bundeer, and I said, "I wish that, no matter what, we'll always be friends." And Holly said, "I wish the same thing."

I'm sitting here in the Tower Room writing while Holly and Tina are getting ready to go to the church supper and the dance afterward. Holly looks really nice in her new blue dress and Tina is helping her fix her hair. Tina acts likes she's gotten over Will. It's hard to tell.

I've figured out that Tina lives in a different country from me. She speaks a different language, dresses differently, cares about different things. I'm not sure I'll ever be able to get a passport to go to her country, but I don't have to be at war with her, either, just because we're different.

Holly is the lucky one. She can travel between both our countries because she can speak both languages. I just have to remember not to be upset when she doesn't happen to be speaking my language.

A Note from the Author

The story of Kiyoshi Mori was inspired by a real person, Takanobu Mitsui (1920–1965), a Japanese student who attended Dartmouth College in Hanover, New Hampshire, from 1939 to 1943. When Pearl Harbor was bombed, Takanobu couldn't get back to his country. Dartmouth's president, Ernest Martin Hopkins, told Takanobu that as long as he was attending Dartmouth, the college would look out for him. (Takanobu's father had attended the college before him and was a loyal alumnus.) Takanobu's diary and letters, as well as letters written by the members of the Dartmouth administration, were made available to me by the Rauner Special Collections Library at Dartmouth College. These materials helped give me a sense of the pressures both on the college and on Takanobu as they wrestled with their decision. The letters Kiyo writes, however, are imagined, as is everything else in this story.

The newspaper article quoted in the story comes from a real article in the *Concord Monitor* written on September 23, 1943.

Two books that were instrumental in helping me understand the atmosphere of the Japanese relocation camps were *The Climate of the Country* by Marnie Mueller (Curbstone Press, 1999) and *Farewell to Manzanar* by Jeanne Wakatsuki Houston and James D. Houston (Houghton Mifflin Books for Children, 2002). I learned a great deal about Civilian Public Service camps from *Another Part of the War: The Camp Simon Story* by Gordon C. Zahn (University of Massachusetts, 1979).

And finally, I wish to express my gratitude to Mary Cash, my editor at Holiday House, whose intelligence and vision have taught me so much.

Time Line

World War I: 1914-1918 (the war that Grandpa fought in)

World War II: 1939-1945 (the war that all the Greenwood brothers were involved in)

- Bombing of Pearl Harbor: Dec. 7, 1941

- Executive Order 9066 signed by Franklin Delano Roosevelt which ordered close to 120,000 Japanese-Americans living in the western part of the U.S. to leave their homes and move to "relocation" centers: 1942

- Opening of Manzanar Relocation Camp: June 2, 1942

- Uprising where soldiers shot into crowd and killed two and injured many: Dec. 1942

- Closing of Manzanar Camp: Nov. 1945

Vietnam War: 1954-1975 (the war that would affect Randy and will)

- 200,000 troops sent to Vietnam: 1965